THE CHRISTMAS STORIES
OF GEORGE MACDONALD

THE CHRISTMAS STORIES OF GEORGE MACDONALD

ILLUSTRATED BY LINDA HILL GRIFFITH

 Chariot Classics

To my dear husband, Bob,
and
our new daughter, Lauren

ACKNOWLEDGMENTS:
Special thanks to the Marion E. Wade Collection, Wheaton College, Wheaton, Illinois, for the use of materials from the George MacDonald collection there, and for the staff's assistance in obtaining these materials.
   "My Uncle Peter" and "The Angel's Song" are abridged from ADELA CATHCART, Loring Publisher, Boston, ca. 1870.
   "A Scot's Christmas Story," or "Papa's Story," is abridged from *Illustrated London News*, December 23, 1865.
   "The Gifts of the Child Christ" is abridged from THE GIFTS OF THE CHILD CHRIST AND OTHER STORIES, Bernhard Tauchnitz Edition, Leipzig, 1882.
   "King Cole" and "The Christmas Child" are reprinted from THE POETICAL WORKS OF GEORGE MACDONALD, VOL. II, Chatto & Windus, Piccadilly, London, 1893.
   "Mary's Lullaby," originally titled "A Christmas Carol," is abridged from POEMS, by George MacDonald, E.P. Dutton & Co., New York, 1890.

THE CHRISTMAS STORIES OF GEORGE MACDONALD
Edited text © 1981 David C. Cook Publishing Co.
Illustrations © 1981 Linda Hill Griffith

Library of Congress Cataloging in Publication Data

MacDonald, George, 1824-1905.
   The Christmas stories of George MacDonald.

   (Chariot classics)
   Contents: My uncle Peter - Mary's lullaby - A Scot's Christmas story - King Cole - The gifts of the Child Christ - The Christmas child - The angel's song.
   1. Christmas—Literary collections. [1. Christmas—Literary collections] I. Griffith, Linda Hill, ill. II. Title.
PR4966.Z57 1981   823'.8   81-68187
ISBN 0-89191-491-9   AACR2

CONTENTS

My Uncle Peter   **7**

Mary's Lullaby   **35**

A Scot's Christmas Story   **39**

King Cole   **61**

The Gifts of the Child Christ   **67**

The Angel's Song   **90**

The Christmas Child   **93**

MY
UNCLE
PETER

"I will tell you the story of my Uncle Peter, who was born on Christmas Day. He was very anxious to die on Christmas Day as well. But I must confess that was rather ambitious of Uncle Peter. Shakespeare is said to have been born on St. George's Day, and there is some ground for believing that he died on St. George's Day. He thus fulfilled a cycle. But we cannot expect that of any but great men. And Uncle Peter was not a great man, though I think I shall be able to show that he was a good man.

"The first remembrance that I have of him is his taking me one Christmas Eve to the largest toy shop in London, and telling me to choose any toy whatever that I pleased. He little knew the agony of choice into which this request of his threw his astonished nephew. If a general right of choice from the treasures of the whole world had been unanimously voted me, it could hardly have cast me into greater perplexity. I wandered about, staring like a distracted ghost at the wealth displayed about me. Uncle Peter followed me with perfect patience.

"As soon as I had made a desperate plunge at decision, my Uncle Peter began buying like a maniac, giving me everything that took his fancy or mine, till we and our toys nearly filled the cab which he called to take us home.

"Uncle Peter was a little, round man, not *very* fat, resembling both in limbs and features an overgrown baby. And I believe the resemblance was not merely an external one. For, though his intellect was quite up to par, he retained a degree of simplicity of character and of tastes that bordered, sometimes, upon the childish.

"'Ah, my dear,' he would say to my mother when she scolded him for making some present far beyond the small means he at that time possessed, 'ah, my dear, you see I was born on Christmas Day.'

"Many a time he would come in from town, where he was a clerk in a merchant's office, with the water running out of his boots, and his umbrella carefully tucked under his arm; and we would know very well that he had given the last coppers he had, for his omnibus home, to some beggar or crossing sweeper, and had then been so delighted with the pleasure he had given, that he forgot to make the best of it by putting up his umbrella. Home he would trudge, in his worn suit of black, with his steel watch chain and bunch of ancestral seals swinging and ringing from his fob, and the rain running into his trousers pockets, to the great endangerment of the health of his cherished old silver watch.

"He was quite poor then, as I have said. I do not think he had more than a hundred pounds a year, and he must have been five and thirty. But Uncle

Peter lived in constant hope and expectation of some unexampled good luck befalling him. 'For,' said he, 'I was born on Christmas Day.'

"He was never married. When people used to jest with him about being an old bachelor, he used to smile, for anything would make him smile. But I was a very little boy indeed when I began to observe that the smile on such occasions was mingled with sadness, and that Uncle Peter's face looked very much as if he were going to cry. But he never said anything on the subject, and not even my mother knew whether he had had any love story or not.

"He lived in lodgings by himself not far from our house. When he was not with us, he was pretty sure to be found seated in his easy chair, for he was fond of his simple comforts, beside a good fire, reading by the light of one candle. He had his tea always as soon as he came home, and some buttered toast or a hot muffin, of which he was sure to make me eat three-quarters if I chanced to drop in upon him at the right hour, which, I am rather ashamed to say, I not unfrequently did.

"Uncle Peter's luck came at last,—at least, he thought it did, when he received a lawyer's letter announcing the *demise* of a cousin of whom he had heard little for a great many years, although they had been warm friends while at school together. The whole of the cousin's fortune was left to Uncle Peter, for the cousin had no nearer relation, and had always remembered him with affection.

"I happened to be seated beside my uncle when the lawyer's letter arrived. Fancy my surprise when my little uncle jumped up on his chair, and thence on the table, upon which he commenced a sort of demoniac hornpipe. But that sober article of furniture declined giving its support to such proceedings for a single moment, and fell with an awful crash to the floor. My uncle was dancing amidst its ruins when he was reduced to an awful sense of impropriety by the entrance of his landlady.

" '*Well!* Mr. Belper,' she began in a surly tone. But, to my astonishment, my uncle was not in the last awed, although I am sure, however much he tried to hide it, that I have often seen him tremble in his shoes at the distant roar of this tigress. But it is wonderful how much courage a pocketful of coins will give.

" 'Take that rickety old thing away,' said my uncle.

" 'Rickety, Mr. Belper! I'm astonished to hear a decent gentleman like you slander the very table as you've eaten off, for the last—'

" 'We won't be precise to a year, ma'am,' interrupted my uncle.

" 'And if you will have little scapegraces of boys into my house to break the furniture, why, them as breaks pays, Mr. Belper.'

" 'Very well. Of course I will pay for it. I broke it myself, ma'am. And if you don't get out of my room I'll—'

"Uncle Peter jumped up once more, and made for the heap of ruins in the middle of the floor. The landlady vanished in a moment, and my uncle threw himself again into his chair, and absolutely roared with laughter.

" 'Shan't we have rare fun, Charlie, my boy?' said he at last, and went off into another fit of laughter.

" 'Why, uncle, what is the matter with you?' I managed to say, in utter bewilderment.

" 'Nothing but luck, Charlie. It's gone to my head. I'm not used to it, Charlie, that's all. I'll come all right by and by.'

"The following morning he gathered together every sixpence he had in the house, and went out of one grocer's shop into another, and out of one baker's shop into another, until he had changed the whole into threepenny pieces. Then he walked to town, as usual, to business.

"But one or two of his friends who were walking the same way, and followed behind him, could not think what Mr. Belper was about. Every crossing that he came to he crossed to the other side. He crossed and recrossed the same street twenty times, they said. But at length they observed that he slipped something into every sweeper's hand as he passed him. It was one of the threepenny pieces. When he walked home in the evening, he had nothing to give.

"At length, after much much maneuvering with the lawyers, who seemed to sympathize with the departed cousin in this, that they, too, would prefer keeping the money till death parted them and it, he succeeded in getting a thousand pounds of it on Christmas Eve.

" 'NOW!' said Uncle Peter, in enormous capitals.

"That night a thundering knock came to our door. We were all sitting in our little dining room,—father, mother, and seven children of us—talking about what we should do next day. The door opened, and in came the most grotesque figure you could imagine. It was seven feet high at least, without any head, a mere walking tree stump, as far as shape went, only it looked soft. The little ones were terrified. But not the bigger ones of us. For from top to toe (if it had a toe) it was covered with toys of every conceivable description, fastened on to it somehow or other.

"We shrieked with delight.

"The figure stood perfectly still, and we gathered round it in a group to

have a nearer view of the wonder. We then discovered that there were tickets on all the articles, and every one of the tickets had one or other of our names upon it.

"This caused a fresh explosion of joy. Nor was it the children only that were thus remembered. A little box bore my mother's name. When she opened it, we saw a real gold watch and chain, and seals and dangles of every sort, of useful and useless kind.

"My father had a silver flute, and to the music of it we had such a dance! The strange figure, now considerably lighter, joined in it without uttering a word. During the dance one of my sisters, a very sharp-eyed little puss, espied about halfway up the monster two bright eyes looking out of a shadowy depth of something like the skirts of a greatcoat. She peeped and peeped, and at length, with a perfect scream of exultation, cried out, 'It's Uncle Peter! It's Uncle Peter!'

"The music ceased. The dance was forgotten. We flew upon him like a pack of hungry wolves. We tore him to the ground; despoiled him of coats, and plaids, and elevating sticks; and discovered the kernel of the beneficent monster in the person of real Uncle Peter, which, after all, was the best present he could have brought us on Christmas Eve. For we had been very dull for want of him, and had been wondering why he did not come.

"Uncle Peter had laid great plans for his birthday, and for the carrying out of them he took me into his confidence—I being now a lad of twelve. He had been for some time perfecting his information about a few of the families in the neighborhood. For he was a bit of a gossip, and did not turn his landlady out of the room when she came in with a whisper of news.

"From her he had learned that a certain artist in the neighborhood was very poor. He made inquiry about him where he thought he could hear more, and finding that he was steady and hardworking, resolved that he should have a more pleasant Christmas than he expected. One other chief outlet for his brotherly love, in the present instance, was a minister and his wife, who had a large family of little children.

"A great part of the forenoon of Christmas Day was spent by my uncle and me in preparations. The presents he had planned were many, but I will only mention two or three of them in particular. For the minister and his family he got a small bottle with a large mouth. This he filled as full of new sovereigns as it would hold, labeled it outside, *Pickled Mushrooms* ('for doesn't it grow in the earth without any seed?' said he), and then wrapped it up like a grocer's parcel.

"For the artist, he took a large shell from his chimneypiece, folded a fifty pound note in a bit of paper, which he tied up with a green ribbon, and inserted the paper in the jaws of the shell, so that the ends of the ribbon should hang out. Then he folded the shell up in paper and sealed it, wrote outside, *Inquire within*, enclosed the whole in a tin box and directed it *With Christmas Day's compliments*. 'For wasn't I born on Christmas Day?' concluded Uncle Peter for the twentieth time that forenoon.

"Nor were the children forgotten. Every house in his street and ours, in which he knew there were little ones, had a parcel of toys and sweet things prepared for it.

"As soon as the afternoon grew dusky, we set out with as many as we could carry. A slight disguise secured me from discovery, my duty being to leave the parcels at the different houses. In the case of the more valuable of them, I was to ask for the master or mistress, and see the packet in safe hands. In this I was successful in every instance. It must have been a great relief to my uncle when the number of parcels were sufficiently diminished to restore to him the use of his hands, for to him they were as necessary for rubbing as a tail is to a dog for wagging.

"We had to go home several times for more, keeping the best till last. When Uncle Peter saw me give the 'pickled mushrooms' into the hands of the lady of the house, he uttered a kind of laugh, which startled the good lady, who was evidently rather alarmed already at the weight of the small parcel. For she said, with a scared look, 'It's not gunpowder, is it?'

"When I looked round I saw my uncle going through a regular series of convolutions, first a dance, then a double-up; then another dance, then another double-up, and so on.

"Everything was a good joke to uncle all that evening.

" 'Charlie,' said he, 'I never had such a birthday in my life before; but, please God, now I've begun, this will not be the last of the sort.'

"When all the parcels were delivered, we walked home together to my uncle's lodgings, where he gave me a sovereign for my trouble. I believe I felt as rich as any of them.

"But now I must tell you the romance of my uncle's life.

"One Christmas Eve we had been occupied, as usual, with the presents of the following Christmas Day. I was helping him to make up parcels, when, from a sudden impulse, I said to him, 'How good you are, uncle!'

" 'Ha! ha! ha!' laughed he, 'That's the best joke of all. Good, my boy! Ha! ha! ha!'

"Then my uncle's face grew suddenly very grave, even sad in its expression. After a pause he resumed, but this time without any laughing, 'Good, Charlie! Why, I'm no use to anybody.'

" 'You do me good, anyhow, uncle,' I answered.

" 'I wish I could be of real, unmistakable use to any one,' he continued. 'But I fear I am not good enough to have that honor done me.'

"Next morning—Christmas Day—he went out for a walk alone, apparently oppressed with the thought with which the serious part of our conversation on the preceding evening had closed. Of course nothing less than a three-penny piece would do for a crossing sweeper on Christmas Day. But one tiny little girl touched his heart so that the usual coin was doubled. Still this did not relieve the heart of the giver sufficiently; for the child looked up in his face in a way, whatever the way was, that made his heart ache. So he gave her a shilling. But he felt no better after that.

"*This won't do,* said Uncle Peter to himself. 'What is your name?'

" 'Little Christmas,' she answered.

" 'Little Christmas!' exclaimed Uncle Peter. 'I see why that wouldn't do now. What do you mean?'

" 'Little Christmas, sir.

" 'What's your father's name?'

" 'I ain't got none, sir.'

" 'But you know what his name was?'

" 'No, sir.'

" 'How did you get your name then? It must be the same as your father's, you know.'

" 'Then I suppose my father was Christmas Day, sir, for I knows of none else. They always calls me Little Christmas.'

"*H'm! A little sister of mine, I see,* said Uncle Peter to himself. 'Well, who's your mother?'

" 'My aunt, sir. She knows I'm out, sir.'

"There was not the least impudence in the child's tone or manner in saying this. She looked up at him with her gypsy eyes in the most confident manner. She had not struck him in the least as beautiful. But the longer he looked at her, the more he was pleased with her.

" 'Is your aunt kind to you?'

" 'She gives me my wittles.'

" 'Suppose you did not get any money all day, what would she say to you?'

" 'Oh, she won't give me a hidin' today, sir, supposin' I gets no more.

You've giv' me enough already, sir. Thank you, sir. I'll change it into ha'pence.'

" 'She does beat you sometimes, then?'

" 'Oh, my!'

"Here she rubbed her arms and elbows as if she ached all over at the thought, and these were the only parts she could reach to rub for the whole.

"*I will,* said Uncle Peter to himself. 'Do you think you were born on Christmas Day, little one?'

" 'I think I was once, sir.'

" 'Will you go home with me?' he said, coaxingly.

" 'Yes, sir, if you will tell me where to put my broom, for I must not go home without it, else aunt would wallop me.'

" 'I will buy you a new broom.'

" 'But aunt would wallop me all the same if I did not bring home the old one for our Christmas fire.'

" 'Never mind. I will take care of you. You may bring your broom if you like, though,' he added, seeing a cloud come over the little face.

" 'Thank you, sir,' said the child. Shouldering her broom, she trotted along behind him, as he led the way home.

"But this would not do, either. Before they had gone twelve paces, Uncle Peter had the child in one hand; and before they had gone a second twelve, he had the broom in the other. And so Uncle Peter walked home with his child and his broom. The latter he set down inside the door, and the former he led upstairs to his room. There he seated her on a chair by the fire, and, ringing the bell, asked the landlady to bring a basin of bread and milk.

"The child sat with her feet wide apart, and reaching halfway down the legs of the chair, and her black eyes staring from the midst of knotted tangles of hair that never felt comb or brush, or were defended from the wind by bonnet or hood. I dare say uncle's poor apartment, with its cases of stuffed birds and its square piano that was used for a cupboard, seemed to her the most sumptuous of conceivable abodes. But she said nothing—only stared. When her bread and milk came, she ate it up without a word, and when she had finished it sat still for a moment, as if pondering what it became her to do next. Then she rose, dropped a curtsy, and said, 'Thank you, sir. Please, sir, where's my broom?'

" 'Oh, but I want you to stop with me, and be my little girl.'

" 'Please, sir, I would rather go to my crossing.' The face of Little Christmas lengthened visibly, and she was upon the point of crying. Uncle Peter saw that he must woo the child before he could hope to win her. The best way seemed to promise her a new frock on the morrow, if she would come and fetch it. Her face brightened at the sound of a new frock.

" 'Will you know the way back, my dear?'

" 'I always know my way anywheres,' answered she. So she was allowed to depart with her cherished broom.

"Uncle Peter took my mother into council upon the affair of the frock. She thought an old one of my sister's would do best. But my uncle had said a *new* frock, and a new one it must be. So next day my mother went with him to buy one, and was excessively amused with his entire ignorance of what was suitable for the child. However, once the frock was purchased, he saw how absurd it would be to put a new frock over such garments as she must have below, and accordingly made my mother buy everything to clothe her completely.

"With these treasures he hastened home, and found poor Little Christmas and her broom waiting for him outside the door, for the landlady would not let her in. This roused the wrath of my uncle to such a degree, that he walked in and gave her notice that he would leave in a week.

"Little Christmas fared all the better for the landlady's unkindness. For my mother took her home and washed her with her own soft hands from head to foot, and then put all the new clothes on her. She looked charming. How my uncle would have managed I can't think. He was delighted at the improvement in her appearance. I saw him turn round and wipe his eyes with his handkerchief.

" 'Now, Little Christmas, will you come and live with me?' said he.

"She pulled the same face, though not quite so long as before, and said, 'I would rather go to my crossing, please, sir.'

"My uncle heaved a sigh and let her go.

"She shouldered her broom, as if it had been the rifle of a giant, and trotted away to her work.

"But next day, and the next, and the next, she was not to be seen at her wonted corner. When a whole week had passed and she did not make her appearance, my uncle was in despair.

" 'You see, Charlie,' said he, 'I am fated to be of no use to anybody, though I was born on Christmas Day.'

"The very next day, however, being Sunday, my uncle found her as he went to church. She was sweeping a new crossing. All her new clothes were gone, and she was more tattered and wretched looking than before. As soon as she saw my uncle she burst into tears.

" 'Look,' she said, pulling up her little frock and showing her thigh with a terrible bruise upon it. '*She* did it.'

"A fresh burst of tears followed.

" 'Where are your new clothes, Little Christmas?' asked my uncle.

" 'She sold them for gin, and then beat me awful. Please, sir, I couldn't help it.'

"The child's tears were so bitter, that my uncle, without thinking, said: 'Never mind, dear; you shall have another frock.'

"Her tears ceased, and her face brightened for a moment. But the weeping returned almost instantaneously with increased violence, and she sobbed out, 'It's no use, sir; she'd only serve me the same, sir.'

" 'Will you come home and live with me, then?'

" 'Yes, please.'

" 'She flung her broom from her into the middle of the street, nearly throwing down a cab horse, betwixt whose forelegs it tried to pass. Then she put her hand in that of her friend and trotted home with him.

"My uncle had by this time got into lodgings with a woman who received the little stray lamb with open arms and open heart. Once more she was washed and clothed from head to foot, and from skin to frock. My uncle never allowed her to go out without him, or some one who was capable of protecting her. He did not think it at all necessary to supply the woman, who might not be her aunt after all, with gin unlimited, for the privilege of rescuing Little Christmas from her cruelty. So he felt that she was in great danger of being carried off, for the sake either of her earnings or her ransom. In fact, some very suspicious-looking characters were several times observed prowling about in the neighborhood.

"Little Christmas was a sweet-tempered, loving child. But the love seemed for some time to have no way of showing itself, so little had she been used to ways of love and tenderness. When we kissed her, she never returned the kiss, but only stared. Yet whatever we asked her to do she would do as if her whole heart was in it, and I did not doubt it was.

"After a few years, when Little Christmas began to be considered tolerably capable of taking care of herself, the vigilance of my uncle gradually relaxed a little. A month before her thirteenth birthday, as near as my uncle could guess, the girl disappeared. She had gone to the day school as usual, and was expected home in the afternoon. (My uncle would never part with her to go to a boarding school, and yet wished her to have the benefit of mingling with

her fellows, and not being always tied to the buttonhole of an old bachelor.) But she did not return at the usual hour.

"My uncle went to inquire about her. She had left the school with the rest. Night drew on. My uncle was in despair. He roamed the streets all night, spoke about his child to every policeman he met, went to the station house of the district, and described her. He had bills printed, and offered a hundred pounds' reward for her restoration. All was unavailing.

"Before the month was out, his clothes were hanging about him like a sack. He could hardly swallow a mouthful, hardly even sit down to a meal. I believe he loved his Little Christmas every whit as much as if she had been his own daughter—perhaps more—for he could not help thinking of what she might have been if he had not rescued her. He felt that God had given her to him as certainly as if she had been his own child. He would get out of bed in the middle of the night, unable to sleep, and go wandering up and down the streets, and into dreadful places, sometimes, to try to find her. But fasting and watching could not go on long without bringing worse things with them. Uncle Peter was seized with a fever, which grew and grew till his life was despaired of. He was very delirious at times, and then the strangest fancies had possession of his brain. Sometimes he seemed to see the horrid woman she called her aunt, torturing the poor child; sometimes it was his old landlady shutting her out in the frost; or himself finding her afterwards, but frozen so hard to the ground that he could not move her to get her indoors. The doctors seemed doubtful, and gave as their opinions a decided shake of the head.

"Christmas Day arrived. In the afternoon, to the wonder of all about him, although he had been wandering a moment before, he suddenly said: 'I was born on Christmas Day, you know. This is the first Christmas Day that didn't bring me good luck.'

"Turning to me, he added: 'Charlie, my boy, it's a good thing *Another* besides me was born on Christmas Day, isn't it?'

" 'Yes, dear uncle,' said I. It was all I could say. He lay quite quiet for a few minutes, when there came a gentle knock to the street door.

" 'That's Chrissy!' he cried, starting up in bed, and stretching out his arms with trembling eagerness. 'And I said this Christmas Day would bring me no good!'

"He fell back on his pillow, and burst into a flood of tears.

"I rushed down to the door, and reached it before the servant. I stared. There stood a girl about the size of Chrissy, with an old, battered bonnet on, and a ragged shawl. She was standing on the doorstep, trembling. She had Chrissy's eyes, too, I thought. But the light was dim now, for the evening was coming on.

" 'What is it?' I said, in a tremor of expectation.

" 'Charlie, don't you know me?' she said, and burst into tears.

" 'Chrissy!' I said, and we were in each other's arms in a moment. I led her upstairs in triumph, and into my uncle's room.

" 'I knew it was my lamb!' he cried, stretching out his arms, and trying to lift himself up, only he was too weak.

"Chrissy flew to his arms. She was very dirty, and her clothes had such a smell of poverty! But there she lay in my uncle's bosom, both of them sobbing, for a long time. When at last she withdrew, she tumbled down on the floor, and there she lay motionless. I was in a dreadful fright, but my mother came in at the moment and got her into a warm bath, and put her to bed.

"In the morning she was much better, though the doctor would not let her get up for a day or two. I think, however, that was partly for my uncle's sake.

"When at length she entered the room one morning, dressed in her own nice clothes, for there were plenty in the wardrobe in her room, my uncle stretched out his arms to her once more and said: 'Ah! Chrissy, I thought I was going to have my own way, and die on Christmas Day; but it would have been one too soon, before I had found you, my darling.'

"It was resolved that, on that same evening, Chrissy should tell my uncle her story.

"After my uncle's afternoon nap was over, Chrissy got up on the bed beside him. I got up at the foot of the bed, facing her, and we had the tea tray and plenty of *etceteras* between us.

" 'Oh! I *am* happy!' said Chrissy, and began to cry.

" 'So am I, my darling!' rejoined Uncle Peter, and followed her example.

" 'So am I,' said I; 'but I don't mean to cry about it.' And then I did.

"We all had one cup of tea, and some bread and butter in silence after this. But when Chrissy had poured out the second cup for Uncle Peter, she began to tell us her story.

" 'It was very foggy when we came out of school that afternoon, as you may remember, dear uncle.'

" 'Indeed I do,' answered Uncle Peter, with a sigh.

" 'I was coming along the way home with Bessie—you know Bessie, uncle—and we stopped to look in at a bookseller's window, where the gas was lighted. It was full of Christmas things already. One of them I thought very

pretty, and I was standing staring at it, when all at once I saw that a big drabby woman had poked herself in between Bessie and me. She was staring in at the window, too. She was so nasty that I moved away a little from her, but I wanted to have one more look at the picture. The woman came close to me. I moved again. Again she pushed up to me. I looked in her face, for I was rather cross by this time.

"A horrid feeling came over me as soon as I saw her. I did not know then why I was frightened. I think she saw I was frightened, for she instantly walked against me, and shoved and hustled me round the corner. Before I knew, I was in another street. It was dark and narrow. Just at that moment a man came from the opposite side and joined the woman. Then they caught hold of my hands, and before my fright would let me speak I was deep into the narrow lane, for they ran with me as fast as they could.

" 'I began to scream, but they said such horrid words that I was forced to hold my tongue. In a minute more they had me inside a dreadful house, where the plaster was dropping away from the walls and the skeleton ribs of the house were looking through. I was nearly dead with terror and disgust. I don't think it was a bit less dreadful to me from having dim recollection of having known such places well enough at one time of my life. I think that only made me the more frightened, because the place seemed to have a claim upon me. What if I ought to be there, after all, and these dreadful creatures were my father and mother!

" 'I thought they were going to beat me at once, when the woman, whom I suspected to be my aunt, began to take off my frock. I was dreadful frightened, but I could not cry. However it was only my clothes that they wanted. But I cannot tell you how frightful it was. They took almost everything I had on, and it was only when I began to scream in despair that they stopped, with a nod to each other, as much as to say, *We can get the rest afterwards.* Then they put a filthy frock on me, brought me some dry bread to eat, locked the door, and left me. It was nearly dark now. There was no fire. All my warm clothes were gone, and I was dreadfully cold. There was a wretched-looking bed in one corner; but I think I would have died of cold rather than get into it. And the air in the place was frightful. How long I sat there in the dark, I don't know.'

" 'What did you do all the time?' said I.

" 'There was only one thing to be done, Charlie. I think that is a foolish question to ask.'

" 'Well, what *did* you do, Chrissy?'

" 'Said my prayers, Charlie,' Chrissy answered.

" 'And then?'

" 'Said them again. Then I tried to get out of the window, but that was of no use; for I could not open it. And it was one story high at least.'

" 'And what did you do next?'

" 'Well, I will tell you. I left my prayers alone, and I began at the beginning. I told God the whole story, as if he had known nothing about it, from when Uncle Peter found me on the crossing down to the minute when I was talking there to him in the dark.

" 'By and by I heard a noise of quarreling in the street, which came nearer and nearer. The door was burst open by someone falling against it. Blundering steps came upstairs. The two who had robbed me, evidently tipsy, were trying to unlock the door. At length they succeeded, and tumbled into the room.

" 'Where is the unnatural wretch,' said the woman, 'who ran away and left her own mother in poverty and sickness?'

" 'O uncle, can it be that she is my mother?' said Chrissy, interrupting herself.

" 'I don't think she is,' answered Uncle Peter. 'She only wanted to vex you, my lamb. But it doesn't matter whether she is or not. You are God's child.'

" 'I am sure of that, uncle. . . . Well, she began groping about to find me, for it was very dark. I sat quite still, except for trembling all over, till I felt her hands on me. When I jumped up, she fell on the floor. She began swearing dreadfully, but did not try to get up. I crept away to another corner. I heard the man snoring, and the woman breathing loud. Then I felt my way to the door, but, to my horror, found the man lying across it on the floor so that I could not open it. Then I believe I cried for the first time. I was nearly frozen to death, and there was all the long night to bear yet.

" 'How I got through it, I cannot tell. It did go away. Perhaps God destroyed some of it for me. But when the light began to come through the window, and show me all the filth of the place, the man and the woman lying on the floor, the woman with her head cut and covered with blood, I began to feel that the darkness had been my friend. I felt this yet more when I saw the state of my own dress, which I had forgotten in the dark. It was an old gown of some woolen stuff, but it was impossible to tell what. I was ashamed that even those drunken creatures should wake and see me in it. But the light *would* come, and it came and came, until at last it waked them up, and the first words were so dreadful! They quarreled and swore at each other and at me,

until I almost thought there couldn't be a God who would let that go on so, and never stop it. But I suppose he wants them to stop, and doesn't care to stop it himself, for he could easily do that of course, if he liked.'

" 'Just right, my darling!' said Uncle Peter, with emotion.

"Chrissy saw that my uncle was too much excited by her story, although he tried *not* to show it, and with wisdom she cut it short.

" 'They did not treat me cruelly, though. The worst was, that they gave me next to nothing to eat. Perhaps they wanted to make me thin and wretched-looking, and I believe they succeeded.

" 'Three days passed this way. I have thought all over it, and I think they were a little puzzled how to get rid of me. They had no doubt watched me for a long time, and now that they had got my clothes, they were afraid. At last one night they took me out. My aunt, if aunt she is, was respectably dressed—that is, comparatively—and the man had a greatcoat on, which covered his dirty clothes. They helped me into a cart, which stood at the door, and drove off. I resolved to watch the way we went. But we took so many turnings through narrow streets before we came out in a main road, that I soon found it was all one mass of confusion in my head; and it was too dark to read any of the names of the streets, for the man kept as much in the middle of the road as possible.

" 'He drove some miles, I should think, before we stopped at the gate of a small house with a big porch, which stood alone. My aunt got out and went up to the house, and was admitted. After a few minutes she returned, and, making me get out, she led me up to the house, where an elderly lady stood, holding the door half open. When we reached it, my aunt gave me a sort of shove in, saying to the lady, "There she is." Then she said to me, "Come now, be a good girl, and don't tell lies," and, turning hastily, ran down the steps, and got into the cart at the gate, which drove off at once the way we had come.

" 'The lady looked at me from head to foot, sternly but kindly, too, I thought, and so glad was I to find myself clear of those dreadful creatures, that I burst out crying. She instantly began to read me a lecture on the privilege of being placed with good people, who would teach me to lead an honest and virtuous life. I tried to say that I had led an honest life. But as often as I opened my mouth to tell anything about myself or my uncle, or, indeed, to say anything at all, I was stopped by her saying, "Now don't tell lies. Whatever you do, don't tell lies." This shut me up quite. I could not speak when I knew she would not believe me.

" 'You may be sure I made haste to put on the nice clean frock she gave me, and, to my delight, found other clean things for me as well. I declare I felt like a princess for a whole day after, notwithstanding the occupation. For I soon found that I had been made over to Mrs. Sprinx, as a servant of all work. I think she must have paid these people for the chance of reclaiming one whom they had represented as at least a great liar. Whether my wages were to be paid to them, or even what they were to be, I never heard. I made up my mind at once that the best thing would be to do the work without grumbling, and do it as well as I could, for that would be doing no harm to any one and give me a better chance of escape.

" 'But though I was determined to get away the first opportunity, and was miserable when I thought how anxious you would all be about me, yet I confess it was such a relief to be clean and in respectable company, that I caught myself singing once or twice the very first day. But the old lady soon stopped that. She was about in the kitchen the greater part of the day till dinner time, and taught me how to cook and save my soul both at once.

" 'I had finished washing up my dinner things, and sat down for a few minutes, for I was tired. I was staring into the fire, and thinking and thinking how I should get away, when suddenly I saw a little boy in a corner of the kitchen, staring at me with great brown eyes. I did not speak to him, but waited to see what he would do. A few minutes passed, and I forgot him. But as I was wiping my eyes, which would get wet sometimes, he came up to me, and said in a timid whisper: 'Are you a princess?'

" 'What makes you think that?' I said.

" 'You have got such white hands,' he answered.

" 'No, I am not a princess.'

" 'Aren't you Cinderella?'

" 'No, my darling, ' I replied. 'But something like her; for they have stolen me away from home and brought me here. I wish I could get away.'

" 'And here I confess I burst into a downright fit of crying.

" 'Don't cry,' said the little fellow, stroking my cheek. 'I will let you out some time. Shall you be able to find your way home all by yourself?'

" 'Yes, I think so,' I answered. But at the same time I felt very doubtful about it, because I always fancied those people watching me. But before either of us spoke again, in came Mrs. Sprinx.

" 'You naughty boy! What business have you to make the servant neglect her work?'

" 'For I was still sitting by the fire, and my arm was round the dear little

30

fellow, and his head was leaning on my shoulder.

" 'She's not a servant, auntie!' cried he, indignantly. 'She's a real princess, though of course she won't own to it.'

" 'What lies you have been telling the boy! You ought to be ashamed of yourself. Come along directly. Get the tea at once, Jane.'

" 'My little friend went with his aunt, and I rose and got the tea. But I felt much lighter hearted since I had the sympathy of the little boy to comfort me. Only I was afraid they would make him hate me. But, although I saw very little of him the rest of the time, I knew they had not succeeded in doing so. As often as he could, he would come sliding up to me, saying, "How do you do, princess?" and then run away, afraid of being seen and scolded.

" 'I was getting very desperate about making my escape, for there was a high wall about the place, and the gate was always locked at night. When Christmas Eve came, I was nearly crazy with thinking that tomorrow was uncle's birthday, and that I should not be with him. But that very night, after I had gone to my room, the door opened, and in came little Eddie in his nightgown, his eyes looking very bright and black over it.

" 'There, princess!' said he. 'There is the key of the gate. Run.'

" 'I took him in my arms and kissed him, unable to speak. He struggled to get free, and ran to the door. There he turned and said, 'You will come back and see me some day. Will you not?'

" 'That I will, I answered.'

" 'That you shall,' said Uncle Peter.

" 'I hid the key, and went to bed, where I lay trembling. As soon as I was sure they must be asleep, I rose and dressed. I had no bonnet or shawl but those I had come in. Though they disgusted me, I thought it better to put them on. But I dared not unlock the street door, for fear of making a noise. So I crept out of the kitchen window, and then I got out at the gate all safe. No one was in sight. So I locked it again, and threw the key over.

" 'But what a time of fear and wandering about I had in the darkness, before I dared to ask anyone the way! It was a bright, clear night, and I walked very quietly till I came upon a great wide common. The sky, and the stars, and the wideness frightened me, and made me gasp at first. I felt as if I should fall away from everything into nothing. But then I thought of God, and grew brave again, and walked on. When the morning dawned, I met a bricklayer going to his work, and found that I had been wandering away from London all the time. But I did not mind that. Now I turned my face towards it, though not the way I had come. I soon got dreadfully tired and faint, and once I think

I fainted quite. I went up to a house, and asked for a piece of bread, and they gave it to me, and I felt much better after eating it. But I had to rest so often, and got so tired, and my feet got so sore, that—you know how late it was before I got home to my darling uncle.'

" 'This shan't happen any more!' said my uncle.

"After tea was over, he wrote a note, which he sent off.

"The next morning, about eleven, as I was looking out of the window, I saw a carriage drive up and stop at our door.

" 'What a pretty little brougham!' I cried. 'And such a jolly horse! Look here, Chrissy!'

"Presently Uncle Peter's bell rang, and Miss Chrissy was sent for. She came down again, radiant with pleasure.

" 'What do you think, Charlie! That carriage is mine—all my own. And I am to go to school in it always. Do come and have a ride in it.'

" 'Where shall we go?' I said.

" 'Let us ask uncle if we may go and see the little darling who set me free.'

"His consent was soon obtained, and away we went. It was a long drive, but we enjoyed it beyond everything. When we reached the house, we were shown into the drawing room. There was Mrs. Sprinx and little Eddie. The lady stared; but the child knew Cinderella at once, and flew into her arms.

" 'I knew you were a princess!' he cried. 'There, auntie!'

"But Mrs. Sprinx had put on an injured look and her hands shook very much. 'Really, Miss Belper, if that is your name, you have behaved in a most unaccountable way. Why did you not tell me, instead of stealing the key of the gate and breaking the kitchen window? A most improper way for a young lady to behave—to run out of the house at midnight!'

" 'You forget, madam,' replied Chrissy, with dignity, 'that as soon as I attempted to open my mouth, you told me not to tell lies. You believed the wicked people who brought me here rather than myself. However, as you will not be friendly, I think we had better go. Come, Charlie!'

" 'Don't go, princess,' pleaded little Eddie.

" 'But I must, for your auntie does not like me,' said Chrissy.

" 'I am sure I always meant to do my duty by you. And I will do so still. Beware, my dear young woman, of the deceitfulness of riches. Your carriage won't save your soul!'

"Chrissy was on the point of saying something rude, as she confessed when we got out, but she did not. She made her bow, turned, and walked away. I followed, and poor Eddie would have done so, too. But he was laid

hold of by the forceful grip of his aunt.

"I confess this was not quite proper behavior on Chrissy's part. But I never discovered that till she made me see it. She was very sorry afterwards, and my uncle feared the brougham had begun to hurt Chrissy already. For she had narrated the whole story to him, and his look first let her see that she had been wrong.

"My uncle went with her afterwards to see Mrs. Sprinx and thank her for having done her best, and to take Eddie such presents as my uncle only knew how to buy for children.

"From that time till now, Chrissy has had no more such adventures. And if Uncle Peter did not die on Christmas Day, it did not matter much, for Christmas Day makes all the days of the year as sacred as itself."

MARY'S LULLABY

Babe Jesus lay in Mary's lap;
The sun shone on his hair;
And this was how she saw, mayhap,
The crown already there.

For she sang: "Sleep on, my little king;
Bad Herod dares not come;
Before thee, sleeping, holy thing,
The wild winds would be dumb.

"For thou art the king of men, my son.
Thy crown I see it plain;
And men shall worship thee, every one,
And cry *Glory! Amen.*"

Babe Jesus opened his eyes so wide!
At Mary looked her Lord.
And Mary ended her song and sighed.
Babe Jesus said never a word.

A SCOT'S
CHRISTMAS
STORY

"Do tell us a story, papa," said a wise-faced little girl, one winter night, as she intermitted for a moment her usual occupation of the hour before bedtime—that, namely, of sucking her thumb.

"Yes, do, papa," chimed in several more children. "It is *such* a long time since you told us a story."

"Well," interposed their papa, "I will try. What shall it be about?"

"Oh! about Scotland," cried the eldest.

"Why do you want a story about Scotland?"

"Because you will like it best yourself, papa."

"I don't want one about Scotland. I'm not a Scotchman, though papa is," cried Dolly, who was five, and one of the youngest. "I'm an Englishman."

"I like Scotch stories," said the sucker of thumbs. "Only I can't understand the curious words. They sound so rough; I never can understand them."

"Well, my darlings, I will tell you one about Scotland, and there shan't be a Scotch word in it. If one single one comes out of my mouth, you may punish me any way you please."

"Oh, that's jolly! How shall we punish papa if he says one Scotch word?"

"Pull his beard!" said Dolly.

"No, that would be rude!" cried three or four.

"Make him pay a fine."

"That's no use; papa's so rich!"

Whereas the chief difficulty papa had in telling the story was the thought of the butcher's bill.

"Make him pay a kiss to each of us for every word!"

"No, that would stop the story!"

"Kiss him to death when it's done!"

"Yes!—yes!—yes—kiss him to death when it's done!"

So it was agreed; and papa began.

"You know, my darlings, there are a great many hills in Scotland, which are green with grass to the very top, and the sheep feed all over them. The tops of these hills are high up and lonely in the air, with the stars above them, and often the clouds round about them like torn garments. In the sunshine, although they do look lonely, they are so bright and beautiful, that all the boys and girls fancy the way to heaven lies up those hills.

"In the winter, on the other hand, they are such wild, howling places, with the hard hailstones beating upon them, and the soft, smothering snowflakes heaping up dreadful wastes of whiteness, that if ever there was a child out on

them he would die with fear, if he did not die with cold. But there are only sheep there when the winter begins.

"The sheep are not very knowing creatures, so they are something better instead. They are wise—that is, they are obedient—creatures, obedience being the very best wisdom. For, they have a shepherd to take care of them, who knows where to take them, especially when a storm comes on.

"Now the shepherd, though he is wise, is not quite clever enough for all that is wanted of him up in those strange, terrible hills; and he needs another to help him. Who do you think helps the shepherd? It is a curious creature with four legs—the shepherd has only two, you know. He is covered all over with long hair of three different colors mixed—black and brown and white—and he has a long nose and a longer tongue. This tongue it is a great comfort to him sometimes to hang out of his mouth as far as ever it will hang. And he has a still longer tail, which is a greater comfort to him yet. I don't know what ever he would do without his tail. For, when his master speaks kindly to him, he is so full of delight, that I think he would die if he hadn't his tail to wag. He lets his gladness off by wagging his tail so that it shan't burst his dear, honest, good dog heart. Ah! there, I've told you. He's a dog, you see. And the very wisest and cleverest of all dogs.

"Well, the shepherd tells the dog what he wants done, and off the dog runs to do it. He can run three times as fast as the shepherd, and can get up and down places much better. I am not sure that he can see better than the shepherd, but I know he can smell better. So that he is just four legs and a long nose to the shepherd, besides the love he gives him, which would comfort any good man.

"One evening, in the beginning of April, the weakly sun of the season had gone down with a pale face behind the shoulder of a hill, and the peat fires upon the hearths of the cottages all began to glow more brightly. On one hearth in particular the peat fire glowed very brightly. There was a pot hanging over it, with supper in it; and a little girl sitting by it, with a sweet, thoughtful face. Her hair was done up in a silken net, for it was the custom with Scotch girls—they wore no bonnet—to have their hair so arranged. She had a bunch of feathers, not in her hair, but fastened to her side by her apron string, in the quill ends of which was stuck the end of one of her knitting needles, while the other was loose in her hand. But both were fast and busy in the loops of a blue-ribbed stocking, which she was knitting for her father.

"He was out on the hills. He had that morning taken his sheep higher up than before, and Nelly knew this. But it could not be long now till she would hear his footsteps and measure the long stride which brought him and happiness home together.

"If you had been in the cottage that night you would have heard a cough every now and then, and would have found that Nelly's mother was lying in a bed in the room—not a bed with curtains, but a bed with doors like shutters. This does not seem a nice way of having a bed. But we would all be glad of the wooden curtains about us at night if we lived in such a cottage, on the side of a hill along which the wind swept like a wild river. Through the cottage it would be streaming all night long. And a poor woman with a cough, or a man who has been out in the cold all day, is very glad of such a place to lie in, and leave the rest of the house to the wind and the fairies.

"Nelly's mother was ill, and there was little hope of her getting well again. What she could have done without Nelly, I can't think. It was so much easier to be ill with Nelly sitting there. For she was a good Nelly.

"After a while Nelly rose and put some peats on the fire and hung the pot a link or two higher on the chain. For she was a wise creature, though she was only twelve, and could cook very well, because she took trouble, and thought about it. Then she sat down to her knitting again.

" 'I wonder what's keeping your father, Nelly,' said her mother.

" 'I don't know, mother. It's not very late yet. He'll be home by and by. You know he was going over the shoulder of the hill today.'

"At length Nelly heard the distant sound of a heavy shoe upon the rock path leading across the furze and brake to their cottage. She always watched for that sound—the sound of her father's shoe, studded thick with broadheaded nails, upon the top of that rock. She started up. But instead of rushing out to meet him, she went to the fire and lowered the pot. Then taking up a wooden bowl, half full of oatmeal neatly pressed down into it, she proceeded to make a certain dish for her father's supper, of which strong Scotchmen are very fond. By the time her father reached the door, it was ready, and set down with a plate over it to keep it hot, though it had a great deal more need, I think, to be let cool a little.

When he entered, he looked troubled. He was a tall man, dressed in rough gray cloth, with a broad, round, blue bonnet, as they call it.

" 'Well, Nelly,' he said, laying his hand on her forehead as she looked up into his face, 'how's your mother?'

"And without waiting for an answer he went to the bed, where the pale face of his wife lay upon the pillow. She held out her thin, white hand to him, and he took it so gently in his strong, brown hand. But, before he had spoken, she saw the trouble on his face, and said, 'What has made you so late tonight, John?'

" 'I was nearly at the fold,' said the shepherd, 'before I saw that one of the lambs was missing. So, after I got them all in, I went back with the dogs to look for him.'

" 'Where's Jumper, then?' asked Nelly, who had been patting the neck and stroking the ears of the one dog, which had followed at the shepherd's heels, and was now lying before the fire, enjoying the warmth none the less that he had braved the cold all day without minding it a bit.

" 'When we couldn't see anything of the lamb,' replied her father, 'I told Jumper to go after him and bring him to the house. He'll have a job of it, poor dog, for it's going to be a rough night. But if any dog can bring him, he will.'

"As the shepherd stopped speaking, he seated himself by the fire and drew the wooden bowl towards him. He lifted his blue bonnet from his head, and said grace, half-aloud, half-murmured to himself. Then he put his bonnet on his head again, for his head was rather bald, and, as I told you, the cottage was a draughty place. Just as he put it on, a blast of wind struck the cottage and roared in the wide chimney. The next moment the rain dashed against the little window of four panes, and fell hissing into the peat fire.

" 'There it comes,' said the shepherd.

" 'Poor Jumper!' said Nelly.

" 'And poor little lamb!' said the shepherd.

" 'It's the lamb's own fault,' said Nelly. 'He shouldn't have run away.'

" 'Ah! yes,' returned her father, 'but then the lamb didn't know what he was about exactly.'

"When the shepherd had finished his supper, he rose and went out to see whether Jumper and the lamb were coming. But the dark night would have made the blackest dog and the whitest lamb both of one color, and he soon came in again. Then he took the Bible and read a chapter to his wife and daughter, which did them all good, even though Nelly did not understand very much of it. He prayed a prayer, and was very near praying for Jumper and the lamb, only he could not quite. And there he was wrong. He should have prayed about whatever troubled him. But he was such a good man that I am almost ashamed of saying he was wrong.

"Just as he came to the *Amen* in his prayer, there came a whine to the door. And there was the lamb, with Jumper behind him. Jumper looked dreadfully wet, and bedraggled, and tired, and the curls had all come out of his long hair. And yet he seemed as happy as a dog could be, and looked up in the face

of the shepherd triumphantly, as much as to say, *Here he is, master!* And the lamb looked scarcely anything the worse, for his thick, oily wool had kept away the wet. And he hadn't been running about everywhere looking for Jumper as Jumper had been for him.

"After Nelly had given him his supper, Jumper lay down by the fire beside the other dog, who made room for him to go next to the glowing peats. The lamb lay down beside him. Then Nelly bade her father and mother and the dogs good night, and went away to bed likewise, thinking the wind might blow as it pleased now, for sheep and dogs and father and all were safe for the whole of the dark, windy hours between that and the morning.

"But there are other winds in the world besides those which shake the fleeces of sheep and the beards of men, or scatter the walls of cottages abroad over the hillsides. There are winds that blow up huge storms inside the hearts of men and women, and blow till the great clouds full of tears rain down from the eyes.

"Nelly lay down in her warm bed, feeling safe and snug. For there was the wind howling outside to make it all the quieter inside; and there was the great, bare, cold hill before the window, which made the bed in which she lay so close, and woolly, and warm.

"Now this bed was separated from her father's and mother's only by a thin partition, and she heard them talking. They had not talked long before that other cold wind that was blowing through their hearts blew into hers, too.

" 'It wasn't the loss of the lamb, John, that made you look so troubled when you came home tonight,' said her mother.

" 'No, it wasn't, Jane, I must confess,'

" 'You've heard something about Willie.'

" 'I can't deny it.'

" 'What is it?'

" 'I'll tell you in the morning.'

" 'I shan't sleep a wink for thinking whatever it can be, John. You had better tell me now. If the Lord would only bring that stray lamb back to his fold, I should die happy—sorry as I should be to leave Nelly and you, my own John.'

" 'Don't talk about dying, Jane. It breaks my heart.'

" 'We won't talk about it, then. But what's this about Willie? And how came you to hear it?'

" 'I was close to the hill road, when I saw James Jamieson, the mail carrier, coming up the hill with his cart. I ran and met him.'

" 'And he told you? What did he tell you?'

" 'Nothing very particular. He only hinted that he had heard, from Wauchope the merchant, that a certain honest man's son—he meant my son, Jane—was going the *wrong road*. And I sat down on a stone, and I heard no more. At least, I could not make sense of what James went on to say. When I lifted my head, James and his cart were just out of sight over the top of the hill. I daresay that was how I lost the lamb.'

"A deep silence followed, and Nelly understood that her mother could not speak. At length a sob and a low weeping came through the boards to her keen mountain ear. But not another word was spoken; and, although Nelly's heart was sad, she soon fell fast asleep.

"Now, Willie had gone to college in Edinburgh, and had been a very good boy for the first winter. They go to college only in winter in Scotland. And he had come home in the end of March and had helped his father to work their little farm, doing his duty well to the sheep and to everything and everybody; for learning had not made him the least unfit for work.

"When winter came, he had gone back to Edinburgh. He ought to have been home a week ago, but he had not come. He had written to say that he had to finish some lessons he had begun to give, and could not be home till the end of April. Now this was so far true that it was not a lie. But there was more in it: he did not want to go home to the lonely hillside—so lonely, that there were only a father and a mother and a sister there. He had made acquaintance with some students who were fonder of drinking whiskey than of getting up in the morning to write abstracts, and he didn't want to leave them.

"Nelly was, as I have said, too young to keep awake because she was troubled; and so, before half an hour was over, was fast asleep and dreaming. And the wind outside, tearing at the thatch of the cottage, mingled with her dream.

"She thought they were out in the dark and the storm, she and her father. But she was no longer Nelly, she was Jumper. Her father said to her, 'Jumper, go after the black lamb and bring him home.'

"Away she galloped over the stones, and through the furze, and across the streams, and up the rocks, and jumped the stone fences, and swam the pools of water, to find the little black lamb. And all the time, somehow or other, the little black lamb was her brother, Willie. Nothing could turn the dog Jumper, though the wind blew as if it would blow him off all his four legs, and off the hill, as one blows a fly off a book. And the hail beat in Jumper's face, as if it

47

would put out his eyes or knock holes in his forehead.

"But it wasn't Jumper; it was Nelly, you know. The dog went on and on, and over the top of the cold wet hill, and was beginning to grow hopeless about finding the black lamb, when, just a little way down the other side, he came upon him behind a rock. He was standing in a miry pool, all wet with rain. Jumper would never have found him, the night was so dark and the lamb was so black, but that he gave a bleat. Whereupon Jumper tried to say *Willie*, but could not, and only gave a gobbling kind of bark. So he jumped upon the lamb, and taking a mouthful of his wool, gave him a shake that made him pull his feet out of the mire, and then drove him off before him, trotting all the way home. When they came into the cottage, the black lamb ran up to Nelly's mother, and jumped into her bed, and Jumper jumped in after him. And then Nelly was Nelly and Willie was Willie, as they used to be, when Nelly would creep into Willie's bed in the morning and kiss him awake.

"When Nelly woke, she was sorry that it was a dream. For Willie was still away, far off on the wrong road, and how ever was he to be got home? Poor black lamb!

"She soon made up her mind. Only how to carry out her idea was the difficulty. All day long she thought about it. And she wrote a letter to her father, telling him what she was going to do. And when she went to her room the next night, she laid the letter on her bed, and putting on her Sunday bonnet and cloak, waited till they should be asleep.

"The shepherd had gone to bed very sad. He, too, had been writing a letter. It had taken him all the evening to write. Nelly had watched his face while he wrote it, and seen how the muscles of it worked with sorrow and pain as he slowly put word after word down on the paper. When he had finished it, and put a seal on it, and addressed it, he left it on the table, and, as I said, went to bed, where he soon fell asleep.

"When Nelly thought he was asleep, she took a pair of stockings out of a chest and put them in her pocket. Then, taking her Sunday shoes in her hand, she stepped gently from her room to the cottage door, which she opened easily, for it was never locked. She found that it was pitch dark. But she could keep the path well enough, for her bare feet told her at once when she was going off it.

"So, dark as it was, she soon reached the road. There was no wind that night, and the clouds hid the stars. She would turn in the direction of Edinburgh, and let the carrier overtake her. For she felt rather guilty, and was

anxious to get on with her important journey.

"After she had walked a good while, she began to wonder that the mail carrier had not come up with her. The fact was that the carrier never left till the early morning. She was not a bit afraid, though, reasoning that, as she was walking in the same direction, it would take him so much the longer to get up with her.

"At length, after walking a long way, she began to feel a little tired, and sat down upon a stone by the roadside. There was a stone behind her, too. She could just see its gray face. She leaned her back against it, and fell fast asleep.

"When she woke, she could not think where she was, or how she had got there. It was a dark, drizzly morning, and her feet were cold. But she was quite dry. The rock against which she fell asleep in the night projected so far over her head that it had kept all the rain off her. She could not have chosen a better place, if she had been able to choose. But the sight around her was very dreary. In front lay a swampy ground, creeping away, dismal and wretched, to the horizon, where a long low hill closed it. Behind her rose a mountain, bare and rocky, on which neither sheep nor shepherd was to be seen. As she came to herself, the fear grew upon her that either she had missed the way in the dark or the carrier had gone past while she slept, either of which was dreadful to contemplate. She began to feel hungry, too, and she had not had the foresight to bring even a piece of oat cake with her.

"It was only dusky dawn yet. There was plenty of time. She would sit down again for a little while; for the rock had a homely look to her. It had been her refuge all night, and she was not willing to leave it. So she leaned her arms on her knees, and gazed out upon the dreary, gray, misty flat.

"Then she rose, and, turning her back on the waste, kneeled down, and prayed to God that, as he taught Jumper to find lambs, he would teach her to find her brother. Thus she fell fast asleep again.

"When she woke once more and turned towards the road, whom should she see standing there but the carrier, staring at her. And his big strong horses stood in the road, too, with their carts behind them. The horses were not in the least surpised. She could not help crying, just a little, for joy.

" 'Why, Nelly, what on earth are you doing here?' said the carrier.

" 'Waiting for you,' answered Nelly.

" 'Where are you going, child?'

" 'To Edinburgh.'

" 'What on earth are you going to do in Edinburgh?'

" 'I am going to my brother, Willie, at the college.'

" 'But the college is over now,' the carrier said.

" 'I know that,' said Nelly.

" 'What's his address, then?' the carrier went on.

" 'I don't know,' answered Nelly.

" 'It's a lucky thing that I know, then. But you have no business to leave home this way.'

" 'Oh! yes, I have.'

" 'I am sure your father did not know of it, for when he gave me a letter this morning to take to Willie, he did not say a word about you.'

" 'He thought I was asleep in my bed,' returned Nelly, trying to smile. But the thought that the carrier had actually seen her father since she left home was too much for her, and she cried.

" 'I can't go back with you now,' said the carrier, 'so you must go on with me.'

" 'That's just what I want.'

"So the carrier made her put on her shoes and stockings, for he was a kind man and had children of his own. Then he pulled out some of the straw that packed his cart, and made her a little bed on the tarpaulin that covered it, just where there was a soft bundle beneath. He lifted her up on it and covered her over with a few empty sacks. There Nelly was so happy and warm and comfortable that, for the third time, she fell asleep.

"When she woke, he gave her some bread and cheese for her breakfast, and some water out of a brook that crossed the road. The rain had ceased and the sun was shining, and the country looked very pleasant. But Nelly thought it a strange country. She could see so much farther! Corn was growing everywhere, there was not a sheep to be seen, and there were many cows feeding in the fields.

" 'Are we near Edinburgh?' she asked.

" 'Oh, no!' answered the carrier. 'We are a long way from Edinburgh yet.'

"And so they journeyed on. The day was flecked all over with sunshine and rain. When the rain's turn came, Nelly would creep under a corner of the tarpaulin till it was over. They slept part of the night at a small town they passed through.

"Nelly thought it a very long way to Edinburgh, though the carrier was kind to her and gave her of everything that he had.

"At length she spied, far away, a great hill, that looked like a couching lion.

" 'Do you see that hill?' said the carrier.

" 'I am just looking at it.'

51

" 'Edinburgh lies at the foot of that hill.'

" 'Oh!' said Nelly, and scarcely took her eyes off it.

"Reaching the brow of a rise, they saw Arthur's Seat (as the carrier said the hill was called) once more, and below it a great jagged ridge of what Nelly took to be broken rocks. But the carrier told her that was the Old Town of Edinburgh. Those fierce-looking splinters on the edge of the mass were the roofs, gables, and chimneys of the great houses.

"The Old Town of Edinburgh is a great marvel to everyone with any imagination at all. And it was nothing less to little Nelly, even when she got into the middle of it. But her heart was so full of its duties towards her black lamb of a brother that the toy shops and the sugar plum shops could not draw it towards their mines of wonder and wealth.

"At length the cart stopped at the public house in the Grassmarket—a wide, open place, with strange old houses all round it, and a huge rock, with a castle on its top, towering over it. There Nelly got down.

" 'I can't go with you till I've unloaded my cart,' said the carrier.

" 'I don't want you to go with me, please,' said Nelly. 'I think Willie would rather not. Please give me father's letter.'

"So the carrier gave her the letter, and got a little boy of the landlady's to show her the way up the West-bow—a street of tall houses, so narrow that you might have shaken hands across it from window to window. From the West-bow they went up a stair into the High-street, and thence into a narrow court, and then up a winding stair, and so came to the floor where Willie's lodging was. There the little boy left Nelly.

"Nelly knocked two or three times before anybody came. When at last a woman opened the door, what do you think the woman did the moment Nelly inquired after Willie? She shut the door in her face with a fierce scolding word. For Willie had vexed her that morning, and she thoughtlessly took her revenge upon Nelly without even asking her a question. Then, indeed, for a moment, Nelly's courage gave way. All at once she felt dreadfully tired, and sat down upon the stair and cried. The landlady was so angry with Willie that she forgot all about the little girl that wanted to see him.

"So for a whole hour Nelly sat upon the stair, moving only to let people pass. She felt dreadfully miserable, but had not the courage to knock again, for fear of having the door shut in her face yet more hopelessly. At last a woman came up and knocked at the door. Nelly rose trembling and stood behind her. The door opened. The woman was welcomed, and she entered. The door was again closing when Nelly cried out in agony, 'Please, ma'am, I want to see my brother Willie!' and burst into sobs.

"The landlady, her wrath having by this time assuaged, was vexed with herself and ashamed that she had not let the child in.

" 'Bless me!' she cried. 'Have you been there all this time? Why didn't you tell me you were Willie's sister? Come in. You won't find him in, though. It's not much of his company we get, I can tell you.'

" 'I don't want to come in, then,' sobbed Nelly. 'Please tell me where he is, ma'am.'

" 'How should I know where he is? At no good, I warrant. But you had better come in and wait, for it's your only chance of seeing him before tomorrow morning.'

"With a sore heart Nelly went in and sat down by the kitchen fire. And the landlady and her visitor sat and talked together, every now and then casting a look at Nelly, who kept her eyes on the ground, waiting with all her soul till Willie should come. Every time the landlady looked, Nelly's sad face went deeper into her heart; so that, before she knew what was going on in herself, she quite loved the child. For she was a kindhearted woman, though she was sometimes cross.

In a few minutes she went up to Nelly and took her bonnet off. Nelly submitted without a word. Then she made her a cup of tea. While Nelly was taking it, the landlady asked her a great many questions. Nelly answered them all; and the landlady stared with amazement at the child's courage and resolution, and thought, *Well, if anything can get Willie out of his bad ways, this little darling will do it.*

"Then she made her go to Willie's bed, promising to let her know the moment he came home.

"Nelly slept and slept till it was night. When she woke, it was dark. But a light was shining through beneath the door. So she rose and put on her frock and shoes and stockings, and went to the kitchen.

" 'You see he's not come yet, Nelly,' said the landlady.

" 'Where can he be?' returned Nelly, sadly.

" 'Oh! he'll be drinking with some of his companions in the public house, I suppose.'

" 'Where is the public house?'

" 'There are hundreds of them, child.'

" 'I know the place he generally goes to,' said a young tradesman who sat by the fire. He had a garret room in the house, and knew Willie by sight. And he told the landlady in a low voice where it was.

" 'Oh! do tell me, please, sir,' cried Nelly. 'I want to get him home.'

" 'You don't think he'll mind you, do you?'

" 'Yes, I do,' returned Nelly confidently.

" 'Well, I'll show you the way if you like. But you'll find it a rough place, I can tell you. You'll wish yourself out of it pretty soon, with or without Willie.'

" 'I won't leave it without him,' said Nelly, tying on her bonnet.

" 'Stop a bit,' said the landlady. 'You don't think I am going to let the child out with nobody but you to look after her?'

" 'Come along, then, ma'am.'

"The landlady put on her bonnet, and out they all went into the street.

"What a wonder it *might* have been to Nelly! But she only knew that she was in the midst of great lights, and carts and carriages rumbling over the stones, and windows full of pretty things, and crowds of people jostling along the pavements. In all the show she wanted nothing but Willie.

"The young man led them down a long dark passage through an archway, and then into a court off the passage, and then up an outside stone stair to a low-browed door, at which he knocked.

" 'I don't much like the look of this place,' said the landlady.

" 'Oh! there's no danger, I dare say, if you keep quiet. They'll never hurt the child. Besides, her brother'll see to that.'

"Presently the door was opened, and the young man asked after Willie. 'Is he in?'

" 'He may be, or he may not,' answered a fat, frowsy woman in a dirty cotton dress. 'Who wants him?'

" 'This little girl.'

" 'Please, ma'am, I'm his sister.'

" 'We want no sisters here.'

"And she proceeded to close the door. I daresay the landlady remembered with shame that she had done the very same that morning.

" 'Come! come!' interposed the young tradesman, putting his foot between the door and the post, 'don't be foolish. Surely you won't keep a child from speaking to her own brother! Why, the queen herself would let her in.'

"This softened the woman a little, and she hesitated, with the latch in her hand.

" 'Mother wants him,' said Nelly. 'She's very ill. I heard her cry about Willie. Let me in.'

"She took hold of the woman's hand, who drew it away hastily, but stepped back, at the same time, and let her enter. She then resumed her place at the door. 'Devil a one of *you* shall come in!' she said, as if justifying the child's admission by the exclusion of the others.

" 'We don't want in, mistress,' said the young man. 'But we'll just see that no harm comes to her.'

" 'D'ye think I'm not enough for that?' said the woman, with scorn. 'Let me see who dares to touch her! But you may stay where you are, if you like. The air's free.'

"So saying, she closed the door, with a taunting laugh.

"The passage in which Nelly found herself was dark. But she saw a light at the further end, through a keyhole, and heard the sounds of loud talk and louder laughter. Before the woman had closed the outer door, she had reached this room. Nor did the woman follow either to guide or prevent her.

"A pause came in the noise. She tapped at the door.

" 'Come in!' cried someone. And she entered.

"Round a table were seated four youths, drinking. Of them one was Willie, with flushed face and flashing eyes. They all stared when the child stood before them, in her odd, old-fashioned bonnet and her little shawl pinned at the throat. Willie stared as much as any of them.

"Nelly spoke first. 'Willie! Willie!' she cried, and would have rushed to him, but the table was between.

" 'What do you want here, Nelly? Who the deuce let you come here?' said Willie, not quite unkindly.

" 'I want you, Willie. Come home with me. Oh! please come home with me.'

" 'I can't, now, Nelly, you see,' he answered. Then, turning to his companions, 'How could the child have found her way here?' he said, looking ashamed as he spoke.

" 'You're fetched. That's all,' said one of them, with a sneer. 'Mother's sent for you.'

" 'Go along!' said another. 'And mind you don't catch it when you get home!'

" 'Nobody will say a word to you, Willie,' interposed Nelly.

" 'Be a good boy, and don't do it again!' said the third, raising his glass to his lips.

"Willie tried to laugh, but was evidently vexed.

" 'What are you standing there for, Nelly?' he said, sharply. 'This is no place for you.'

" 'Nor for you either, Willie,' returned Nelly, without moving.

" 'We're all very naughty, aren't we, Nelly?' said the first.

" 'Come and give me a kiss, and I'll forgive you,' said the second.

" 'You shan't have your brother. So you may trudge home again without him,' said the third.

"And then they all burst out laughing, except Willie.

" 'Do go away, Nelly, ' he said, angrily.

" 'Where am I to go to?'

" 'Where you came from.'

" 'That's home,' said Nelly. 'But I can't go home tonight, and I daren't go home without you. Mother would die. She's very ill, Willie. I heard her crying last night.'

"It seemed to Nelly at the moment that it was only last night she left home.

" 'I'll just take the little fool to my lodgings and come back directly,' said Willie, rather stricken at this mention of his mother.

" 'Oh! yes. Do as you're bid!' they cried, and burst out laughing again. For they despised Willie because he was only a shepherd's son, although they liked to have his company because he was clever.

"But Willie was angry now. 'I tell you what,' he said. 'I'll go when and where I like.'

"Two of them were silent now, because they were afraid of Willie. For he was big and strong. The third, however, trusting to the others, said, with a nasty sneer, 'Go with its little sister to its little mammy!'

"Now Willie could not get out, so small was the room and so large the table, except one or other of those next him rose to let him pass. Neither did. Willie therefore jumped on the table, kicked the tumbler of the one who had last spoken into the breast of his shirt, jumped down, took Nelly by the hand, and left the house.

" 'The rude boys!' said Nelly. 'I would never go near them again, if I was you, Willie.'

"But Willie said never a word, for he was not pleased with Nelly or with himself or with his *friends*.

"When they got into the house, he said, abruptly, 'What's the matter with mother, Nelly?'

" 'I don't know, Willie. But I don't think she'll ever get better. I'm sure father doesn't think it either.'

"Willie was silent for a long time. Then he said, 'How did you come here, Nelly?'

"And Nelly told him the whole story.

" 'And now you'll come home with me, Willie.'

" 'It was very foolish of you, Nelly. To think you could bring me home if I didn't choose!'

" 'But you do choose, don't you, Willie?'

" 'You might as well have written,' he said.

"Then Nelly remembered her father's letter, which the carrier had given her. And Willie took it, and sat down, with his back to Nelly, and read it through. Then he burst out crying, and laid his head on his arms and went on crying. Nelly got upon a bar of the chair—for he was down on the table—and leaned over him, and put her arms round his neck, and said, crying herself all the time, 'Nobody said a word to the black lamb when Jumper brought him home, Willie.'

"And Willie lifted his head, and put his arms round Nelly, and drew her face to his, and kissed her as he used to kiss her years ago.

"And I needn't tell you anything more about it."

"Oh! yes, papa. Tell us how they got home."

"They went home with the carrier the next day."

"And wasn't his father glad to see Willie?"

"He didn't say much. He held out his hand with a half-smile on his mouth, and a look in his eye like the moon before a storm."

"And his mother?"

"His mother held out her arms, and drew him down to her bosom, and stroked his hair, and prayed God to bless Willie, her boy."

"And Nelly? Weren't they glad to see Nelly?"

"They made more of Willie than they did of Nelly."

"And wasn't Nelly sorry?"

"No. She never noticed it—she was so busy making much of Willie, too."

"But I hope they didn't scold Nelly for going to fetch Willie?"

"When she went to bed that night, her father kissed her and said, 'The blessin' o' an auld father be upo' ye, my wee bairn!'

"There's Scotch," now exclaimed the whole company.

And in one moment papa was on the floor, buried beneath a mass of children.

KING COLE

King Cole he reigned in Aureoland,
But the sceptre was seldom in his hand.

Far oftener was there his golden cup—
He ate too much, but he drank all up!

To be called a king and to be a king,
That is one thing and another thing!

So his majesty's head began to shake,
And his hands and his feet to swell and ache.

The doctors were called, but they dared not say
"Your majesty drinks too much Tokay;"

So out of the king's heart died all mirth,
And he thought there was nothing good on earth.

Then up rose the fool, whose every word
Was three parts wise and one part absurd—

"Nuncle," he said, "never mind the gout;
I will make you laugh till you laugh it out."

King Cole pushed away his full gold plate;
The jester he opened the palace gate,

Brought in a cold man, with hunger grim,
And on the dais edge seated him;

Then caught up the king's own golden plate,
And set it beside him: oh, how he ate!

And the king took note, with a pleased surprise,
That he ate with his mouth and his cheeks and his eyes,

With his arms and his legs and his body whole.
The king laughed aloud from his heart and soul,

Then from his lordly chair got up,
And carried the man his own gold cup:

The goblet was deep and wide and full,
The poor man drank like a cow at a pool.

Said the king to the jester, "I call it well done
To drink with two mouths instead of one!"

Said the king to himself, as he took his seat,
"It is quite as good to feed as to eat!

"It is better, I do begin to think,
To give to the thirsty than to drink!

"And now I have thought of it," said the king,
"There might be more of this kind of thing!"

The fool heard. The king had not long to wait:
The fool cried aloud at the palace gate;

The ragged and wretched, the hungry and thin,
Loose in their clothes and tight in their skin,

Gathered in shoals till they filled the hall,
And the king and the fool they fed them all;

And as with good things their plates they piled
The king grew merry as a little child.

On the morrow, early, he went abroad
And sought poor folk in their own abode—

Sought them till evening foggy and dim,
Did not wait till they came to him;

And every day after did what he could,
Gave them work and gave them food.

Thus he made war on the wintry weather,
And his health and the spring came back together.

But, lo, a change had passed on the king,
Like the change of the world in that same spring!

His face had grown noble and good to see,
And the crown sat well on his majesty.

Now he ate enough, and ate no more,
He drank about half what he drank before,

He reigned a real king in Aureoland,
Reigned with his head and his heart and his hand.

All this through the fool did come to pass.
And every Christmas Eve that was,

The palace gates stood open wide
And the poor came in from every side,

And the king rose up and served them duly,
And his people loved him very truly.

THE GIFTS
OF THE
CHILD CHRIST

"My hearers, we grow old," said the preacher solemnly. "The wind of the world sets for the tomb. Happy the man who shall then be able to believe that old age itself is the chastening of the Lord, a sure sign of his love and his fatherhood."

It was the first Sunday in Advent. But "the chastening of the Lord" came into almost every sermon the man preached.

Eloquent! But after all, can this kind of thing be true? said to himself a man of about thirty, who sat decorously listening. For many years he had thought he believed in God's love and fatherhood—but of late he was not so sure.

Beside him sat his wife, in her new winter bonnet, her pretty face turned up toward the preacher. But her eyes revealed that she was not listening. She was much younger than her husband—hardly twenty, indeed.

In the upper corner of the pew sat a pale-faced child about five, sucking her thumb and staring at the preacher.

The sermon over, the three walked home. The husband looked gloomy, and his eyes sought the ground. The wife looked more smiling than cheerful, and her pretty eyes went hither and thither. Behind them walked the child—steadily facing forward.

In Wimborne Square, a region of large, commonplace houses, they stopped, and entered one of them. The door of the dining room was open, showing the table laid for their Sunday dinner. The gentleman passed on to the library behind it, the lady went up to her bedroom, and the child a stage higher to the nursery.

It was half an hour to dinner. Mr. Greatorex sat down, drummed with his fingers on the arm of his easy chair, took up a book of arctic exploration, threw it again on the table, got up, and went to the smoking room. Again he seated himself, took a cigar, and smoked gloomily.

Having reached her bedroom, Mrs. Greatorex took off her bonnet, and stood for ten minutes turning it round and round.

Little Sophy—or, as she called herself, Phosy—found her nurse Alice in the nursery. But Alice was lost in the pages of a certain London weekly, and did not even look up when the child entered. With some effort Phosy drew off her gloves, and with more difficulty untied her hat. Then she took off her jacket, smoothed her hair, and retreated to a corner. There a large shabby doll lay upon her little chair. She took it up, disposed it gently upon the bed, seated herself in its place, got a little book from where she had left it under the chair, smoothed down her skirts, and began simultaneously to read.

68

But she did not read far. Her thoughts went back to a phrase which had haunted her ever since first she went to church: "Whom the Lord *loveth*, he chasteneth."

I wish he would chasten me, she thought for the hundredth time.

The small Christian had no suspicion that her whole life had been a period of chastening, or punishment—that few children indeed had to live in such a sunless atmosphere as hers.

Alice threw down the newspaper, gazed from the window into the backyard of the next house, saw nothing but an elderly manservant brushing a garment, and turned upon Sophy.

"Why don't you hang up your jacket, miss?" she said, sharply.

The little one rose, opened the wardrobe door wide, carried a chair to it, fetched her jacket from the bed, clambered up on the chair, and, leaning far forward to reach a peg, tumbled right into the bottom of the wardrobe.

"You clumsy!" exclaimed the nurse angrily, and pulling her out by the arm, shook her.

Alice was not generally rough to her, but there were reasons today.

Phosy crept back to her seat, pale, frightened, and a little hurt. Alice hung up the jacket, closed the wardrobe, and, turning, contemplated her own pretty face and neat figure in the glass opposite. The dinner bell rang.

"There, I declare!" she cried, and wheeled round on Phosy. "And your hair not brushed yet, miss! Will you ever learn to do a thing without being told it? Thank goodness, I shan't be plagued with you long! But I pity her as comes after me, I do!"

The maid seized Phosy roughly by the arm, and brushed her hair with an angry haste that made the child's eyes water and herself feel a little ashamed at the sight of them.

"How could anybody love such a troublesome chit?" Alice said.

Another sigh was the poor little damsel's only answer. She looked very white and solemn as she entered the dining room.

Mr. Greatorex was a merchant in the city. Some six years before, he had married to please his parents. And a year before, he had married to please himself. His first wife had intellect, education, and heart, but little individuality—not enough to reflect the individuality of her husband. The consequence was, he found her uninteresting. But in truth his wife had great capabilities, only they had never ripened. When she died, a fortnight after giving birth to Sophy, her husband had not a suspicion of the large amount of undeveloped power that had passed away with her.

Sophy was so like her both in countenance and manner that he was too constantly reminded of her unlamented mother. Love alone gives insight, and the father took her merely for a miniature edition of the volume which he seemed to have laid aside forever in the dust.

A year ago, he had married to please himself. Letty Merewether was the daughter of a bishop. She had been born tolerably innocent, and had grown up more than tolerably pretty. In his suit of her, Greatorex had prospered—perhaps too easily. He loved the girl, or at least loved the modified reflection of her in his own mind. But they had not been married many days before the scouts of advancing disappointment were upon them. Augustus resisted manfully for a time. He tried to interest Letty in one subject after another—tried her first with political economy. In that instance, when he came home to dinner he found that she had not got beyond the first page of the book he had left with her. He saw his mistake, and tried her with poetry. But it was to her equally uninteresting. He tried her next with the elements of science, but with no better success.

I believe she read a chapter of the Bible every day, but the only books she read with any real interest were novels of a sort that Augustus despised. Besides these books, there was nothing in her universe but fashion, dress, calls, the park, other-peopledom, concerts, plays, churchgoing.

It was no wonder, therefore, that Augustus was at length compelled to admit himself disappointed in his wife. He was too much of a man not to cherish a certain tenderness for her, but he soon found to his dismay that it had begun to be mingled with a shadow of contempt. He stopped later and later at business, and when he came home spent more and more of his time in the smoking room, where by and by he had bookshelves put up. Occasionally he would accept an invitation to dinner and accompany his wife, but he detested evening parties. When Letty, who never refused an invitation if she could help it, went to one, he remained at home with his books. But his power of reading began to diminish. He became restless and irritable. Something kept gnawing at his heart. There was a sore spot in it.

On her part, Letty, too, had her grief, which, unlike Augustus, she did not keep to herself. More than one of her friends offered her the soothing assurance that Augustus was only like all other men. Women were but their toys, which they cast away when weary of them.

And all the time poor little Phosy was left to the care of Alice, a clever, careless, good-hearted, self-satisfied damsel, who, although seldom so rough in her behavior as we have just seen her, abandoned the child almost entirely

to her own resources. It was often Phosy sat alone in the nursery, wishing the Lord would chasten her—because then she would know he loved her.

The first course of this particular Sunday dinner was nearly over ere Augustus had brought himself to ask, "What did you think of the sermon today, Letty?"

"Not much. I am not fond of finery. I prefer simplicity."

Augustus held his peace bitterly.

Presently she spoke again. "Gus, dear, couldn't you make up your mind for once to go with me to Lady Ashdaile's tomorrow? I am getting quite ashamed of appearing so often without you."

"There is another way of avoiding that unpleasantness," remarked her husband drily. "Stay with me at home."

"You cruel creature!" returned Letty playfully. "But I must go this once, for I promised Mrs. Holden."

"You know, Letty," said her husband, after a little pause, "it gets of more and more consequence that you should not fatigue yourself. By keeping such late hours in such stifling rooms you are endangering *two* lives, your own and that of our unborn child. Remember that, Letty. If you stay at home tomorrow, I will come home early, and read to you all the evening."

"Gussy, that *would* be charming. You *know* there is nothing in the world I should enjoy so much. But this time I really mustn't."

She launched into a list of all the great nobodies and small somebodies who were to be there, and whom she positively must see. It might be her only chance.

Phosy say in a corner, listened and understood. Neither father nor mother spoke to her till they bade her good night. Neither saw the hungry heart under the mask of the still face.

The next morning Alice gave her mistress warning that she planned to leave. It was quite unexpected, and Letty looked at her aghast.

"Alice," she said at length, "you're never going to leave me at such a time!"

"I'm sorry it don't suit you, ma'am, but I must."

"I have always been kind to you," resumed her mistress.

"I'm sure, ma'am, I never made no complaints!" returned Alice, but as she spoke she drew herself up straighter than before.

"Then what is it?"

"The fact is, ma'am," answered the girl, almost fiercely, "I cannot any longer endure a state of domestic slavery."

"I don't understand you a bit better," said Mrs. Greatorex, trying, but in

73

vain, to smile, and therefore looking angrier than she was.

"I mean, ma'am—an' I see no reason as I shouldn't say it, for it's the truth—there's a worm at the root of society where one yuman bein's got to do the dirty work of another. I don't mind sweepin' up my own dust, but I won't sweep up nobody else's. I ain't a goin' to demean myself no longer! There!"

"Leave the room, Alice," said Mrs. Greatorex. When, with a toss and a flounce, the young woman had vanished, Letty burst into tears of anger and annoyance.

That night Letty was taken ill. Her husband called Alice, and ran himself to fetch the doctor. For some hours she seemed in danger, but by noon was much better. The greatest care was necessary.

As soon as she could speak, Letty told Augustus of Alice's warning, and he sent for her.

She stood before him with flushed cheeks and flashing eyes.

"I understand, Alice, you have given your mistress warning," he said gently.

"Yes, sir."

"Your mistress is very ill, Alice."

"Yes, sir."

"Come now, Alice," said her master, "what's at the back of all this? You have been a good, well-behaved, obliging girl till now. I am certain you would never be like this if there weren't something wrong somewhere."

"Something wrong, sir! No, indeed, sir! Except you call it wrong to have an old uncle as dies and leaves ever so much money—thousands on thousands, the lawyers say."

"And does it come to you then, Alice?"

"I get my share, sir. He left it to be parted even between his nephews and nieces."

"Why, Alice, you are quite an heiress, then!" returned her master, scarcely, however, believing the thing so grand as Alice would have it. "But don't you think now it would be rather hard that your fortune should be Mrs. Greatorex's misfortune?"

"Well, I don't see as how it shouldn't," replied Alice. "It's mis'ess's fortun' as has been my misfortun'—ain't it now, sir? An' why shouldn't it be the other way next?"

"I don't quite see how your mistress's fortune can be said to be your misfortune, Alice."

"Anybody would see that, sir, as wasn't blinded by class prejudices."

"Class prejudices!" exclaimed Mr. Greatorex, in surprise at the word.

"It's a term they use, I believe, sir! But it's plain enough that if mis'ess hadn't 'a' been better off than me, she wouldn't ha' been able to secure my services—as you calls it. . . . All I say, sir, is—it's my turn now; and I ain't goin' to be sit upon by no one. I know my dooty to myself."

"I didn't know there was such a duty, Alice," said her master.

Something in his tone displeased her.

"Then you know now, sir," she said, and bounced out of the room.

The next moment, however, ashamed of her rudeness, she reentered, saying, "I don't want to be unkind, sir, but I must go home. I've got a brother that's ill, too, and wants to see me. If you don't object to me goin' home for a month, I promise you to come back and see mis'ess through her trouble—as a friend, you know, sir."

"But just listen to me first, Alice," said Mr. Greatorex. "I've had something to do with wills in my time, and I can assure you it is likely to be more than a year before you can touch the money. You had much better stay where you are till your uncle's affairs are settled. You don't know what may happen. There's many a slip between cup and lip, you know."

"Oh! it's all right, sir. Everybody knows the money's left to his nephews and nieces, and me and my brother's as good as any."

"I don't doubt it. Still, if you'll take my advice, you'll keep a sound roof over your head till another's ready for you."

Alice only threw her chin in the air, and said almost threateningly, "Am I to go for the month, sir?"

"I'll talk to your mistress about it," answered Mr. Greatorex, not at all sure that such an arrangement would be for his wife's comfort.

But the next day Mrs. Greatorex had a long talk with Alice, and the result was that on the following Monday she was to go home for a month, and then return for two months more at least. What Mr. Greatorex had said about the legacy had had its effect. Besides, her mistress had spoken to her with pleasure in her good fortune.

About Sophy no one felt any anxiety. She was no trouble to anyone, and the housemaid would see to her.

On Sunday evening, Alice's lover, having heard, not from herself, but by a side wind, that she was going home the next day, made his appearance in Wimborne Square, somewhat perplexed—both at the move, and at her leaving him in ignorance of the same. He was a cabinetmaker in an honest shop.

Full of the sense of her new superiority, Alice met him draped in an indescribable strangeness. John Jephson felt, at the very first word, as if her voice came from the other side of the English Channel.

"Alice, my dear," he said—for John was a man to go straight at the enemy, "what's amiss? What's come over you? Here I find you're goin' away, and ne'er a word to me about it! What have I done?"

Alice's chin alone made reply. She waited the fitting moment, with splendor to astonish, and with grandeur to subdue her lover. To tell the sad truth, she was no longer sure that it would be well to encourage him on the old footing. Was she not standing on the brink of the brook that parted serfdom from gentility?

"Alice, my girl!" began John again, in expostulatory tone.

"*Miss Cox*, if you please, John Jephson," interposed Alice.

"What on earth's come over you?" exclaimed John, with the first throb of rousing indignation. "I wouldn't take no liberties with a lady, Miss Cox; but if I might be so bold as to arst the joke of the thing——"

"Joke, indeed!" cried Alice. "Do you call a dead uncle and ten thousand pounds a joke?"

"God bless me!" said John. "You don't mean it, Alice?"

"I do mean it, and that you'll find, John Jephson. I'm goin' to bid you good-bye tomorrer."

"Whoy, Alice!" exclaimed honest John, aghast.

"It's truth, I tell ye," said Alice.

"And for how long?"

"That depends," returned Alice, who did not care to lessen the effect of her communication by mentioning her promised return for a season. "It ain't likely," she added, "as a heiress is a goin' to act the nussmaid much longer."

"But Alice," said John, "you don't mean as how this 'ere money—dang it all!—as how it's to be all over between you and me? You *can't* mean that, Alice!" ended the poor fellow, with a choking in his throat.

"Arst yourself, John Jephson," answered Alice, "whether it's likely a young lady of fortun' would be keepin' company with a young man as didn't know how to take off his hat to her in the park?"

John rose, grievously wounded. "Good-bye, Alice," he said, taking the hand she did not refuse. "Ye're throwin' from ye what all yer money won't buy."

She gave a scornful little laugh, and John walked out of the kitchen.

At the door he turned with one lingering look. But there was no sign of softening in Alice. She turned scornfully away, and no doubt enjoyed her triumph to the full.

The next morning she went away.

That year Christmas Eve fell upon a Monday. The day before, Letty not feeling very well, her husband thought it better not to leave her, and gave up going to church. Phosy was utterly forgotten, but she dressed herself, and at the usual hour appeared with her prayer book in her hand ready for church. When her father told her that he was not going, she looked so blank that he took pity upon her, and accompanied her to the church door, promising to meet her as she came out. Phosy sighed from relief as she entered, for she had a vague idea that by going to church to pray for it, she might move the Lord to chasten her. At least he would see her there, and might think of it. She had never had such an attention from her father before, never such dignity conferred upon her as to be allowed to appear in church alone, sitting in the pew by herself like a grown damsel.

What the preacher said I need not even partially repeat. It is enough to mention a certain deposit from the stream of his eloquence carried home in her mind by Phosy. From some of his sayings about the birth of Jesus into the world, into the family, into the individual human bosom, she got it into her head that Christmas Day was not a birthday like she had herself. Instead, in some wonderful way, the baby Jesus was born every Christmas Day afresh. What became of him afterwards she did not know. Indeed she had never yet thought to ask how it was that he could come to every house in London as well as No. 1, Wimborne Square.

Her father forgot the time over his book, but so entranced was her heart with the expectation of Jesus' promised visit, now so near—the day after tomorrow—that, if she did not altogether forget to look for him as she stepped down the stair from the church door to the street, his absence caused her no uneasiness. Just as she reached home, he opened the door in tardy haste to redeem his promise, and she looked up at him with a solemn, smileless repose upon her face. Walking past him without change in the rhythm of her motion, she marched stately up the stairs to the nursery. I believe the center of her hope was that when the baby came she would beg him on her knees to ask the Lord to chasten her.

When dessert was over, her mother on the sofa in the drawing room, and her father in an easy chair, Phosy crept out of the room and away again to the nursery. There she reached up to her little bookshelf, and, full of the sermon

as spongy mists are full of the sunlight, took a volume of stories narrating the visit of the Christ child, laden with gifts, to a certain household, and sat down with it by the fire, the only light she had. When the housemaid, suddenly remembering she must put her to bed, hurried to the nursery, she found her fast asleep in her little armchair, her book on her lap.

On Christmas Eve the church bells were ringing through the murky air of London, whose streets lay flaring and steaming below. The brightest of their constellations were the butcher's shops, with their shows of prize beef. Around them, the eddies of the human tides were most confused and knotted. But the toy shops were brilliant also. To Phosy they would have been the treasure caves of the Christ child—all mysteries, all with insides to them— boxes, and desks, and windmills, and hens with chickens, and who could tell what all? In every one of those shops her eyes would have searched for the Christ child, the giver of all their wealth. For to her *he* was everywhere that night.

John Jephson was out in the middle of all the show, drifting about in it. He saw nothing that had pleasure in it, his heart was so heavy. He never thought once of the Christ child, or even of the Christ man, as the giver of anything. For poor John this Christmas held no promise. With all his humor, he was one of those people who, having once loved, cannot cease. During the fortnight he had scarce had a moment's ease from the sting of his Alice's treatment.

It had also been a troubled fortnight for Mrs. Greatorex. She wished much that she could have talked to her husband more freely, but she had not learned to feel at home with him. Yet he had been kinder and more attentive than usual all the time, so much so that Letty thought with herself—if she gave him a boy, he would certainly return to his first devotion. She said *boy*, because anyone might see he cared little for Phosy.

That evening she was seated alone in the drawing room, her husband having left her to smoke his cigar, when the butler entered and informed her that Alice had returned, but was behaving so oddly that they did not know what to do with her. Asking wherein her oddness consisted and learning that it was mostly in silence and tears, she felt considerable curiosity to know what it was. She told him to send her upstairs.

The moment Alice entered the drawing room, she fell on her knees at the foot of the couch on which her mistress lay, covered her face with her hands, and sobbed grievously. She was pale and worn, and had a hunted look—was in fact a mere shadow of what she had been. For a time her mistress found it impossible to quiet her so as to draw her story from her.

"Oh, ma'am!" she burst out at length. "How ever *can* I tell you? You will never speak to me again. Little did I think such a disgrace was waiting me!"

"It was no fault of yours if you were misinformed," said her mistress, "or that your uncle was not the rich man you fancied."

"Oh, ma'am, there was no mistake there! He was more than twice as rich as I fancied. If he had only died a beggar, and left things as they was!"

An agonized burst of fresh weeping followed, and it was with prolonged difficulty, and by incessant questioning, that Mrs. Greatorex at length drew from her the following facts.

Before Alice and her brother could receive the legacy to which they laid claim, it was necessary to produce certain documents, the absence of which led to the unavoidable publication of a fact previously known only to a living few—namely, that the father and mother of Alice Hopwood had never been married. This fact deprived them of the smallest claim on the legacy, and fell like a millstone upon Alice and her pride. She was, in her own judgment at least, no longer the respectable member of society she had hitherto been justified in supposing herself. Worst of all, she had insulted her lover as beneath her notice, and the next moment had found herself too vile for his.

When Mrs. Greatorex had given her what consolation she found handy, and at length dismissed her, the girl, unable to endure her own company, sought the nursery, where she caught Sophy in her arms and embraced her with fervor. Never in her life having been the object of any such display of feeling, Phosy was much astonished. When Alice had set her down and she had resumed her seat by the fireside, Phosy went on staring for a while. Then she rose and went to Alice, where she sat looking into the fire, unconscious of the scrutiny she had been undergoing, and, looking up in her face, took her thumb out of her mouth, and said, "Is the Lord chastening Alice? I wish he would chasten Phosy."

Her face was calm as that of the Sphinx. There was no mist in the depth of her gray eyes, not a cloud on the wide heaven of her forehead.

Was the child crazed? What could the atom mean, with her big eyes looking right into her? Alice never had understood her. But there was a something in Phosy's face besides its calmness and unintelligibility. What it was Alice could never have told—yet it did her good. She lifted the child on her lap. There Phosy soon fell asleep. Alice undressed her, laid her in her crib, and went to bed herself.

But, weary as she was, she had to rise again before she got to sleep. Her mistress was again taken ill. Doctor and nurse were sent for in hot haste. Hansom cabs came and went throughout the night, like noisy moths to the one lighted house in the street. There were soft steps within, and doors were gently opened and shut. The waters of death had risen and filled the house.

Toward morning they were ebbing slowly away. Letty did not know that her husband was watching by her bedside. The street was quiet now. So was the house. Most of its people had been up throughout the night, but now they had all gone to bed except the strange nurse and Mr. Greatorex.

It was the morning of Christmas Day, and little Phosy knew it in every cranny of her soul. She was not of those who had been up all night, and now she was awake, early and wide. The moment she awoke she was speculating: He was coming today. How would he come? Where should she find the baby Jesus? And when would he come? In the morning, or the afternoon, or in the evening? Could such a grief be in store for her as that he would not appear until night, when she would be again in bed? But she would not sleep till all hope was gone. Would everybody be gathered to meet him, or would he show himself to one after another, each alone? Then her turn would be last, and oh, if he would come to the nursery! But perhaps he would not appear to her at all. For was she not one whom the Lord did not care to chasten?

Expectation grew and wrought in her until she could lie in bed no longer. Alice was fast asleep. It must be early, but whether it was yet light or not, she could not tell for the curtains. Anyhow she would get up and dress. Then she would be ready for Jesus whenever he should come. True, she was not able to dress herself very well, but he would know, and would not mind. She made all the haste she could, and was soon attired after a fashion.

She crept out of the room and down the stair. The house was very still. What if Jesus should come and find nobody awake? Would he go again and give them no presents? Perhaps she ought to wake them all, but she dared not without being sure.

On the last landing above the first floor, she saw, by the low gaslight at the end of the corridor, an unknown figure pass the foot of the stair. Could she have anything to do with the marvel of the day? When Phosy reached the bottom of the stair, she saw the figure disappearing in her stepmother's room. That she did not like. It was the one room into which she could not go. But, as the house was so still, she would search everywhere else. If she did not find Jesus, she would then sit down in the hall and wait for him.

The room next the foot of the stair, and opposite her stepmother's, was the spare room, with which she associated ideas of state and grandeur. Where better could she begin than at the guest chamber?

There! Could it be? Through the chink of the scarce-closed door she saw light. Either he was already there or they were expecting him. Far exalted above all dread, she peeped modestly in, and then entered. Beyond the foot of the bed, a candle stood on a little low table, but nobody was to be seen. There was a stool near the table. She would sit on it by the candle, and wait for him.

But ere she reached it, she caught sight of something upon the bed that drew her thither. She stood entranced. *Could* it be?—It *might* be. Perhaps Jesus had left it there while he went into her mamma's room with something for her. The loveliest of dolls ever imagined! She drew nearer. The light was low, and the shadows were many. She could not be sure what it was. But when she had gone close up to it, she concluded with certainty that it was a doll—perhaps intended for her—but beyond doubt the most exquisite of dolls. She dragged a chair to the bed, got up, pushed her little arms softly under it, and drawing it gently to her, slid down with it.

When she felt her feet firm on the floor, filled with the solemn composure of holy awe, she carried the gift of the child Jesus to the candle, that she might better admire its beauty and know its preciousness. But the light had no sooner fallen upon it than a strange undefinable doubt awoke within her. Whatever it was, it was the very essence of loveliness—the tiny darling with its alabaster face and its delicately modeled hands and fingers! A long night-gown covered all the rest.

Was it possible? Could it be? Yes, indeed! it must be—it could be nothing else than a *real* baby! What a goose she had been! Of course it was baby Jesus himself! For was not this his very own Christmas Day on which he was always born?

One shudder of bliss passed through her, and in an agony of possession she clasped the baby to her great heart—then at once became still with the satisfaction of eternity, with the peace of God. She sat down on the stool, near the little table, with her back to the candle, that its rays should not fall on the eyes of the sleeping Jesus and wake him. There she sat, lost in the very majesty of bliss, at once the mother and the slave of the Lord Jesus.

She sat for a time still as marble waiting for marble to awake, heedful as tenderest woman not to rouse him before his time, though her heart was swelling with the eager petition that he would ask his Father to be as good as to chasten her. As she sat, she began to model her face to the likeness of his, that she might understand his stillness—the absolute peace that dwelt on his countenance. But as she did so, again a sudden doubt invaded her. Jesus lay so very still—never moved, never opened his pale eyelids! And now set thinking, she noted that he did not breathe. She had seen babies asleep, and their breath came and went—their little bosoms heaved up and down, and sometimes they would smile, and sometimes they would moan and sigh. But Jesus did none of these things. Was it not strange? And then he was cold—oh, so cold!

A blue silk coverlid lay on the bed. She half rose and dragged it off, and contrived to wind it around herself and the baby. Sad at heart, very sad, but undismayed, she sat and watched him on her lap.

Meantime the morning of Christmas Day grew. The light came and filled the house. The sleepers slept late, but at length they stirred. Alice awoke last—from a troubled sleep, in which the events of the night mingled with her own lost condition and destiny. After all Polly had been kind, she thought, and got Sophy up without disturbing her.

She had been but a few minutes downstairs, when a strange and appalling rumor made itself somehow known through the house, and every one hurried up in horrible dismay.

The nurse had gone into the spare room, and missed the little dead thing she had laid there. The bed was between her and Phosy, and she never saw her. The doctor had been sharp with her about something the night before. She now took her revenge in suspicion of him, and after a hasty and fruitless visit of inquiry to the kitchen, hurried to Mr. Greatorex.

The servants crowded to the spare room. When their master, incredulous indeed, yet shocked at the tidings brought him, hastened to the spot, he found them all in the room, gathered at the foot of the bed. A little sunlight filtered through the red window curtains, and gave a strange pallid expression to the flame of the candle, which had now burned very low. At first he saw nothing but the group of servants, silent, motionless, with heads leaning forward, intently gazing. He had come just in time: another moment and they would have ruined the lovely sight. He stepped forward, and saw Phosy, half-shrouded in blue, the candle behind illuminating the hair she had found too rebellious to the brush, and making of it a faint halo about her head and white face. She had pored on the little baby's face until she knew death, and now she sat a speechless mother of sorrow, bending in the dim light of the tomb over the body of her holy infant.

How it was I cannot tell, but the moment her father saw her she looked up, and the spell of her dumbness broke.

"Jesus is dead," she said, slowly and sadly, but with perfect calmness. "He is dead," she repeated. "He came too early, and there was no one up to take care of him, and he's dead—dead—dead!"

But as she spoke the last words, the frozen lump of agony gave way; the well of her heart suddenly filled, swelled, overflowed; the last word was half-sob, half-shriek of utter despair and loss.

Alice darted forward and took the dead baby tenderly from her. The same moment her father raised the little mother and clasped her to his bosom. Her arms went round his neck, her head sank on his shoulder, and sobbing in grievous misery, yet already a little comforted, he bore her from the room.

"No, no, Phosy!" they heard him say. "Jesus is not dead, thank God. It is only your little brother that hadn't life enough, and is gone back to God for more."

Weeping, the women went down the stairs. Alice's tears were still flowing when John Jephson entered. Her own troubles forgotten in the emotion of the scene she had just witnessed, she ran to his arms and wept on his bosom.

John stood as one astonished.

"O Lord! this *is* a Christmas!" he sighed at last.

"Oh, John!" cried Alice, and tore herself from his embrace, "I forgot! You'll never speak to me again, John! Don't do it, John."

And with the words she gave a stifled cry, and fell to weeping again, behind her two shielding hands.

"Why, Alice! You ain't married, are you?" gasped John, to whom that was the only possible evil.

"No, John, and never shall be. A respectable man like you would never think of looking twice at a poor girl like me!"

"Let's have one more look anyhow," said John, drawing her hands from her face. "Tell me what's the matter. If there's anything can be done to right you, I'll work day and night to do it, Alice."

"There's nothing *can* be done, John," replied Alice, and would again have floated out on the ocean of her misery, but in spite of sobs and tears, she held on and told her tale, not even omitting the fact that when she went to the eldest of the cousins and "demeaned herself" to beg a little help for her brother, who was dying of consumption, he had all but ordered her out of the house, swearing he had nothing to do with her or her brother, and saying she ought to be ashamed to show her face.

86

"And that when we used to make mud pies together!" concluded Alice with indignation. "There, John! You have it all, " she added. "—And now?"

With the word she gave a deep, humbly questioning look into his honest eyes.

"Is that all, Alice?" he asked.

"Yes, John. Ain't it enough?"

"More'n enough," answered John. "I swear to you, Alice, you're worth to me ten times what you would ha' been, even if you'd ha' had me, with ten thousand pounds in your ridicule. Why, my woman, I never saw you look one 'alf so 'an'some as you do now!"

"But the disgrace of it, John!" said Alice, hanging her head.

"Let your father and mother settle that betwixt 'em, Alice. 'Tain't none o' my business. Please God, we'll do different. When shall the wedding be, my girl?"

"When you like, John," answered Alice, without raising her head.

When she had withdrawn herself from the too rigorous embrace with which he received her consent, she remarked, "I do believe, John, money ain't a good thing! Sure as I live, with the very wind o' that money, the devil entered into me. Didn't you hate me, John? Speak the truth now."

"No, Alice. I did cry a bit over you, though."

"I do believe if that money hadn't been took from me, I'd never ha' had you, John. Ain't it awful to think on?"

"Well, no. O' coorse! How could ye?" said Jephson—with reluctance.

"Now, John, don't ye talk like that, for I won't stand it. Don't you go for to set me up again with excusin' of me. I'm a nasty conceited cat, I am—and all for nothing but mean pride."

"Mind ye, ye're mine now, Alice. An' what's mine's mine, an' I won't have it abused. I knows you are twice the woman you was afore, and all the world couldn't gi' me such another Christmas box—no, not if it was all gold watches and roast beef."

When Mr. Greatorex returned to his wife's room, and thought to find her asleep as he had left her, he was dismayed to hear sounds of soft weeping from the bed. Some tone or stray word, never intended to reach her ear, had been enough to reveal the truth concerning her baby.

"Hush! hush!" he said, with more love in his heart than had moved there for many months, and therefore more in his tone than she had heard for as many. "If you cry, you will be ill. Hush, my dear!"

In a moment, ere he could prevent her, she had flung her arms around his neck as he stooped over her.

"Husband! husband!" she cried, "is it my fault he died?"

"You behaved perfectly," he returned. "No woman could have been braver."

"Ah, but I wouldn't stay at home when you wanted me."

"Never mind that now, my child."

At the word she pulled his face down to hers.

"I have *you*, and I don't care," he added.

"*Do* you care to have me?" she said, with a sob that ended in a loud cry. "Oh! I don't deserve it. But I *will* be good after this. I promise you I will."

"Then you must begin now, my darling. You must lie perfectly still, and not cry a bit, or you will go after the baby, and I shall be left alone."

She looked up at him with such a light in her face as he had never dreamed of there before. He had never seen her so lovely. Then she withdrew her arms, repressed her tears, smiled, and turned her face away. He put her hands under the clothes, and in a minute or two she was again fast asleep.

That day, when Phosy and her father had sat down to their Christmas dinner, he rose again, and taking her up as she sat, chair and all, set her down close to him, on the other side of the corner of the table. It was the first of a new covenant between them, the father's eyes having been suddenly opened to her character and preciousness, as well as to his own neglected duty in regard to her. And every day, as he looked in her face and talked to her, it was with more and more respect for what he found.

Nor was little Sophy his only comfort. Through their common loss and her husband's tenderness, Letty began to grow a woman. And her growth was the more rapid because her husband no longer desired to make her adopt *his* tastes, and judge with his experiences, but, as became the elder and the tried, entered into her tastes and experiences.

As soon as she was able to bear it, he told her the story of the dead Jesus, and with the tale came to her heart love for Phosy. She had lost a son for a season, but she had gained a daughter for ever.

Such were the gifts the Christ child brought to one household that Christmas. And the days of the mourning of that household were ended.

THE
ANGEL'S
SONG

From heaven above I come to you,
To bring a story good and new:
Of goodly news so much I bring,
I cannot help it, I must sing.

To you a child is come this morn,
A child of holy maiden born,
A little babe, so sweet and mild,
It is a joy to see the child.

'Tis little Jesus, whom we need
Us out of sadness all to lead:
He will himself our Saviour be,
And from all sinning set us free.

Here come the shepherds, whom we know;
Let all of us right gladsome go,
To see what God to us hath given—
A gift that makes a stable heaven.

Take heed, my heart! Be lowly. So
Thou seest him lie in manger low:
That is the baby sweet and mild,
That is the little Jesus child.

Ah, Lord! the maker of us all,
How hast thou grown so poor and small?
There thou liest on withered grass—
The supper of the ox and ass.

Were the world wider many fold,
And decked with gems and cloth of gold,
'Twere far too mean and narrow all
To make for thee a cradle small.

Rough hay, and linen not too fine
Are the silk and velvet that are thine.
Yet as if they were thy kingdom great,
Thou liest in them in royal state.

Ah, little Jesus, lay thy head
Down in a soft, white, little bed
That waits thee in this heart of mine,
And then this heart is always thine.

Such gladness in my heart would make
Me dance and sing for thy sweet sake.
Glory to God in highest heaven,
For he to us his Son hath given!

THE
CHRISTMAS
CHILD

"Little one, who straight hast come
   Down the heavenly stair,
Tell us all about your home,
   And the Father there."

"He is such a one as I—
   Like as like can be.
Do his will, and, by and by,
   Home and him you'll see."

94